Light And Dark

21 Short

C.G. Harris

PublishNation
www.publishnation.co.uk

To my family, who are above all things to me

Preface

Of these stories: I hope that some make you laugh, that others make you think or surprise you with their endings - but most importantly, I hope they all give you pleasure.

If they succeed in this, I will be one happy writer.

CONTENTS

Preface

About the Author

SUSPICION

Let me ask you this – was there a time when you couldn't believe your eyes? I mean, you *literally* could not believe what you were seeing? If there was, did your jaw drop or did you just rub your eyes and swear to yourself? I'm telling you now I did all three when I saw a certain guy push his wife overboard.

It happened so quickly, and he was so *natural* about it – murder being such a quaint, inconsequential thing, of course – that I felt I just had to be mistaken, right? One casual glance round, one quick motion to grasp both ankles, and a swift heave, and she was gone. Then, a turn and stroll along the windswept deck and – get this – an audacious nod and smile to the steward as he passed him, and he was away. The trouble with something like that is it's so outrageous it just can't be true - can it?

I know that it *can* be true, and although I was drunk, I was feeling just sober enough not to want to get myself killed – so I stayed right where I was, hidden in the shadow of a hanging lifeboat, the large, motorised kind with plenty of room that they always use on cruise ships these days (lessons learned from the *Titanic*, right?). I didn't detach myself from the wall holding me up till the man was gone – and I mean *well* gone. Then, I stumbled to the stern and peered over the rails.

I could see nothing in the water but waves, churned to a white hue by the thrust of the engines. The waves settled and quickly merged into the blackness of the Pacific - it was difficult to see anything beyond them. Even the dim light from a crescent moon didn't help, given that it was partially hidden by long threads of cloud being shunted along in the sky by the south easterly wind. If there really had been a woman she was gone, left swiftly behind in a cold, vast and indifferent sea. It was a desolate way to go and I began to quickly sober up and ask myself what I could do, and what I should do.

Ok, firstly – had I actually seen what I thought I had? I shook my head to clear it and ran my fingers back through the hair I had left, then massaged my temples with both hands. I came to the conclusion that I had seen it indeed. I closed my eyes and tried hard to recollect something that had happened only a few seconds ago, but that already seemed like a distant dream.

The night was warm. Of course, it is cold in Alaska, but in August, with the ship two days out from Ketchikan on the return down to Seattle on the US mainland, the air temperature was a tourist-acceptable 66 °F. The woman had been wearing neither a jacket nor a coat, and I had recognised the same belted, light blue dress with white stripes on that she had been wearing when she boarded with her husband seven days before. Her striking yellow hair had set her apart, and I recalled thinking at that time how it seemed incongruous with her middle age. They had seemed happy enough, but I guess I was wrong – one of them had been very unhappy for sure.

Two other questions struck me. You may think it odd, but the first one – *how the hell is he going to get away with this?* – arose before the second, which should have been the most important – *can she be saved?* I guess it was less than a minute from the moment the woman disappeared until that question entered my head, and it suddenly made me turn and look for that steward, though I knew that the cold shock of the water followed by hypothermia was just as likely to kill her as drowning by the time help could get to her. I saw him on the upper deck smoking an illicit cigarette - the end glowed red and amber and a wisp of white smoke spun upwards and was shredded quickly by the wind. I was about to raise my arm and yell, when I realised I was not alone – there he stood, the *devoted husband*, silent and still, not five feet away. He was looking at me curiously, although in as unconcerned fashion as you like, and though my blood temperature seemed to drop a few degrees and my stomach muscles tightened, I immediately tried to adopt his casual manner, then, deciding it was best to take refuge in my drunkenness, slouched against the rails.

"Whoa, you seem the worse for wear." He said this in a cultured west coast voice with an amused look in his eyes that I didn't really like, but which I pretended not to notice.

"Seasickness," I answered, though the sea was only mildly choppy.

"Possibly a martini or two as well," he laughed. "Although my wife does suffer from seasickness."

"Is she sick now?" It was a foolhardy dig. I was befuddled and scared, but, irrational as it may seem, I suddenly felt annoyed at his

2

nonchalance.

He shrugged his shoulders. They looked large in his tight, lightweight navy blazer. He looked kind of generally out of shape, even for a late middle-aged man, but I knew that he had strong arms – you can't throw someone overboard in a single heave without them, I know that much.

"She's lying down in our cabin right now."

There, I felt that doubt creep up again. He was as cool as could be – surely, I couldn't be mistaken? But when I closed my eyes, I recalled that tiny cry of surprise – not fear, but surprise – that had come from her trusting mouth and that had dissolved into the night as its owner spun and tumbled downwards. I decided I needed to get to my cabin, not only to straighten my thoughts, but because I was afraid he would realise that I wasn't as drunk as I was pretending to be. For me, that wouldn't prove to be a good thing for him to know.

I muttered a good night, and he raised a hand and nodded as I made my way along the deck towards the centre of the ship. I opened the door to the stairs leading to the cheaper cabins below-decks and chanced a glance back. I immediately wished that I hadn't; although the deck was not particularly well lit, I could see him leaning casually against the stern rails, with the now uncovered moon floating behind him. His eyes were hidden in the shadows, but I could tell that he was looking directly at me. He was rubbing his chin slowly, as if pondering over something – I could guess what it was.

*

Sleep did not come easily, or the morning quickly. Tomorrow, there would be one full day of cruising left. I had a feeling that it would be filled with self-doubt and indecision mixed with an awful lot of anxiety, and accompanied by fear. I lay on my berth throughout the night, looking out of a porthole through which I could see little but dismal clouds passing by. It was probably my imagination that heavy footsteps occasionally stopped outside my door.

The cabin was small, making me feel oppressed – the one my wife and I had shared a few years ago had been larger, almost grandiose, in comparison. It was not the same ship, of course; this one was of middling size, and revisiting our last trip together was a somewhat bitter, almost masochistic reminiscence for me, because she had left me shortly after. But I had certainly not expected to be lying where I

3

was, thinking of another man's wife and the possibility that he had purposefully killed her. I finally slept.

*

I was once told that no matter how bad things looked during the day, they look a hell of a lot worse at night. The reverse must be true of the morning because when I woke and saw blue sky through that same porthole and heard passengers conversing, seemingly without a care, as they made their way to an early breakfast in one of the diners, my concerns yet again dwindled to a kind of nagging doubt. In all honesty, I had no idea what to do. In any event, although I wasn't sure that modern vessels still had them, I decided that I was not going to hide away below decks like a rat on a ship.

I risked a look in the mirror and saw what I had expected to see after the night I'd had – a slightly jowly face of fifty-two, eyes somewhat bloodied, with dark circles beneath them. I admitted to myself, though, that I was used to seeing my eyes that way – wine drunk to excess tended to have that effect. I reflected that it had been my wife who had often driven me to it. I began to feel a kinship with that guy if his wife was anything like mine.

I showered, then dressed in fresh but un-ironed cream linen slacks and a white shirt, and brushed my hair. I remembered how it had once been, longer and abundant. I was disappointed but resigned to the fact that was no longer the case. Getting older is a bummer for us all, but I wasn't looking too bad. I left the cabin and headed for breakfast, pretending that nothing was amiss. It was only when I thought of the guy looking at me the previous night that I felt the occasional prickle on my neck.

The woman first spoke to me at the buffet table. She was young - but not too young -of an age when it isn't totally out of the question that someone as good looking as her would want to strike up a conversation. It was, after all, a cruise ship with over 800 passengers on board; people do speak to other people... don't they?

The thing was, I didn't think anything of it, and we conversed over croissants and coffee. She was interesting enough – and interested in me enough – for me to allow myself to forget the previous night for a short while, and when she suggested meeting for a drink that evening, I accepted. We finished breakfast and walked out on deck, where I watched as she sashayed away, dark-haired and slim – someone,

4

somewhere, was a lucky guy.

For the rest of the day, I alternated between curiosity and apprehension, sometimes on a crowded deck – I felt safer around people – and at other times in my locked cabin, sharing a bottle of cheap Chablis with myself. I saw no sign of the husband.

The next day, we were to dock in Seattle after a round trip – Juneau, Glacier Bay, Ketchikan and then home. I wanted…needed… to see what would happen when we disembarked. I felt that I couldn't be wrong about what I had seen – but many people, including the crew and the passengers, had seen and conversed with both him and his wife on the journey. He'd said she was in their cabin, but he had to leave the ship – how could he do that without his wife? I put off deciding what to do until the following day.

My head swam, only partly as a consequence of the wine, and it had not cleared entirely by the time of my date, but I made my way to the bar that looked out over a dark, balmy sea upon which the ship fairly glided, as if it couldn't wait to get home to port. The woman sat at a stool with a vodka martini, and although the bar was crowded, she had saved me a place. A glass of wine – full, but not for long – awaited me.

I guess flattery and attention after being deprived of a woman's company for long is enough to turn many a man's head – and I don't except mine. She was fun, she was pretty. There comes a time in an evening when confidences flow along with the alcohol, and a couple of times, I almost told her what I'd seen the previous night. I stopped myself, but only because I didn't want her to think I was mad or a drunk, and at least one of these was true. In any event, we made progress on other fronts. We exchanged cell phone numbers and addresses, and promised to look each other up. It was the usual vague thing that vacationers say and do - if I'd been hoping, in my middle-aged head, for something more tonight, it wasn't going to happen.

We went out on deck, and I said goodnight and watched her walking away – it was a pleasurable sight. She passed a man nearby who was leaning over the rails, looking out at the sea. I did the same. I think it was my imagination, but I thought that I could see the distant orange and yellow lights of mainland US winking at us in welcome, although I knew we were still many hours away.

I looked across at the man, and it was *him* – he looked back at me.

He was dressed smartly but casually, and I put his age at close to mine; perhaps, we weren't really so different - apart from the odd case of homicide. We stared at each other for a moment or two, and I felt he still had this slightly undecided air about him. He slowly walked away. I shivered and retreated to my cabin.

*

I slept better than the night before, perhaps because I knew that things were coming to a head. When I woke and went upstairs, our ship had wended its way through Puget Sound, and we were coming into Elliot Bay. The Port of Seattle looked, as you might expect, full of bustle; the long-winded aggravation of disembarkation loomed before us. My luggage had been colour coded, and I waited up on deck for my group to be called. During my wait, I scanned the gangway on the designated lower deck fervently for the husband; I was certain he would have had a suite, which takes priority over single cabins when leaving the ship.

Well, my jaw dropped open, and I swore yet again – the guy seemed to have a habit of making me do that - when I saw him and his wife, with a carry-on piece of luggage each, mingling with the crowds as they pushed and shoved along with the best of them. Her yellow hair blazed in the sunshine, and she was wearing that same light blue, belted dress, or something very like it. There seemed to be something of a kerfuffle, and her husband was arguing with one of the stewards, but she swiped her cruise card to debark. It was only when she was jostled and she dropped her bag and lifted her sunglasses, the better to pick it up, that I saw it was my pretty companion from the night before – my jaw dropped even further. She looked up, and that feeling you get when you know something is inevitable hit me. She put her glasses over her head with her right hand and looked directly at me for a longish moment. Smiling, she pulled her glasses back down, nudging the man. He suddenly stopped arguing, and, with an angry gesture, he turned away from the steward, and the pair of them strode casually to the exit terminal. It was the last that I saw of them.

I certainly needed a drink. The interminable debarkation made me wait, which was just as well, because by the time I had claimed my baggage, I had decided to take a cab to *Bar Harbor*, a ten-minute drive away, and finally think this one through.

I sat in the bar and ordered the most expensive bottle of Chablis that I could afford – a *Grand Cru Bougros* – filled a glass and raised it. Before I drank, I thought of my wife, whose behavior had turned me into the drunk I was, and who had then left me because of it. I thought then of that guy who, for whatever reason, had taken his future into his own hands. All it had taken was a blonde wig, a blue dress, a lover to wear them, of course, and a diversion at debarkation while she swiped the wife's cruise card with her own.

I drank to him. I wouldn't be telling, and not just because, cold blooded as it was, I couldn't judge him awfully for doing what he had done. Nor because I had a suspicion, and my grudging respect, that he had committed the perfect homicide.

Why then? Because that guy sure knows how to plan a murder. And now he has my address.

THE NEW SAMARITAN

I always say *"You can't judge a book by its cover."*

I was reminded of this as I sat in a shop doorway late last night. God, that wind was bitter. It whipped in and out and around me and froze my fingers and the stump of my leg and went deep inside to my bones. Don't let anyone tell you a doorway can be snug; it may keep some of the rain out but the cold – it just gets to you; it won't be denied. Mind you, I only had two blankets – one I sat on, but still the stone chilled me, and the other I pulled tight around my shoulders. I had to hold it there with one hand to stop it from sliding down. My other hand was outstretched – I can stay like that for hours when the weather is good.

What was I saying? Yes... appearances.

The last train had rattled in. I had been waiting for this before I could bugger off to somewhere warmer for the night - there are usually a good few late-night revellers returning home, hopefully pissed enough to throw me a couple of quid.

I was cursing when only three groups came out of the station but my hopes were raised when the first was a young couple. Then I looked at their eyes.

Let me tell you something I learned in Helmand (I personally spell it HELLmand by the way). You rarely get close to the enemy – it's all bombs and IEDs, all long-range stuff. But it happened once, and as the madness unfolded around me and the gunfire deafened me and shook my senses all to pieces, I found myself grappling with a young bloke who was madder than a dervish and had the zeal of a Believer. Nutter. He wasn't afraid – not until I stunned him and looked him in the eye. It was either him or me, and I had no choice – but for a moment I could see right into his soul and realised what drove him; I didn't like what I saw but I learned this – look hard enough at the eyes and you *will* see what lies back there.

This young couple was well dressed and well heeled – a night at the theatre no doubt. I watched their eyes carefully as they looked sideways at me. There was no joy there for me, I knew straightaway, and I suspected there was precious little joy between them either, despite their holding hands. They acted as though I wasn't there.

The second group was a bunch of old biddies dressed up to the nines; I thought they looked like churchgoers. They would surely be up in the morning early when the bells tolled, and I hoped Charity would trump Faith and Hope when they saw me. Not a bit of it; they passed by on the other side of the road, clearly not inspired by the Good Samaritan they must have read about in their Bible classes.

I must admit I had no hopes for the third group; the gang of three kids had been idling around, finishing their cans of beer and jostling each other. They looked the aggressive type, but aggression held no fears for me anymore; only hopelessness bothered me.

When they approached me, my hand was still outstretched, and one of them put an empty beer can on it, and they all laughed. A second, I could see, was readying himself to pour beer on my head; I gave him the Helmand stare, and he changed his mind and called me a tosser instead. The third lad pushed him onwards, a bit rough like, and told him to pack it in and when they had gone a few steps, turned back and stood in front of me. He didn't look much; skinny, with rough, short cropped hair, but turns out he was an angel in ripped jeans and a parka.

He looked down at my stump and then at me, and he said, "My Grandad was in the war." His voice was quiet when he said this.

"Desert Rats."

Of course, he meant the Second World War - but war is war.

I looked closely into his eyes, and I could see his Grandad staring out at me; a man who kept his medals in a drawer and hid his heroic light under a bushel.

The boy ripped the can from my hand and threw it fiercely on the floor and placed a tenner there instead. He ran to join his friends, and when the traffic lights turned red, he turned and gave me a thumbs- up, crossed the road, and was gone.

I will say, for a minute I was elevated from the grime…and I forgot all about the wind.

9

LIGHTHOUSE EDDY

It is a truth well acknowledged in my country that fact is stranger than fiction; I care to believe that this wisdom stands true the world over.

I've travelled much, both believing and disbelieving the things I had seen. I have been often elated and sometimes disturbed. Run the gauntlet between truth and lies as you read and make of my story what you will – only know that I insist it happened just as I relate, and that I wish it had not.

To call your country and the things in it *quaint* does it a great disservice. The lighthouse at Spirren Head was not quaint; the narrow sand spit on which it lay, reaching out into an austere North Sea and curling back like a beckoning finger into the Humber estuary, even less so. I wondered what my countrymen in cosmopolitan Boston, Massachusetts, USA, would call this bleak place, and I guessed quaint would not be the word that they would use – no sir.

That being said, I reckon that all lighthouses, by their nature, brooding constantly as they do over scenes of potential and actual tragedy, will always have a melancholic air. I did not hold its bleakness against it; I merely looked across the bay and felt a compulsion to look out from those rocks to where a surly sea and sky merged with a darkening acceptance of the early dusk.

To this end, I made my way on foot through the village of Essingham, which was a single, unlit street with cramped, glowering houses on either side and the sole feature of redemption being a public house just lighting up; you can bet that I had it in mind to call in when I came back that way.

I found the spit was a combination of sand and shingle, at times narrowing to 50 yards across with mudflats on the landward side; the occasional gull rose and twisted in the wind, and I, in turn, stepped out and braced myself against it, suddenly chilled and wondering why the lighthouse remained unlit.

It was three miles to the southernmost tip, far enough to call it lonely, if not outright isolated. When I reached the base of the lighthouse, it was what we call a damp squib, the door and all windows boarded. Quite evidently, it was no longer in use – I took a turn around it all the same, and on the seaward side, a moon, half- hearted until now, spilled light through the length of its column, such that my shadow was cast against grainy, flaking walls, elongated and distorted. A small wooden structure stood to the side, which, by its design, looked as though it might once just have housed an occupant or two; the whole prospect became suddenly grim to my writer's mind. The dark, defunct tower stretched into the night sky in such a forlorn manner, its railed apex shrouded on one side by shadow and the other by moonlight, that I suddenly felt the need for company, and I would take my chances on whether that was yet another cheerless Yorkshireman; despite the darkening, intermittent cloud, I made my way back along the spit more hurriedly than I had come.

The Wayfarer was the kind of public house that delights us Americans, a kind of a throwback to pre-*bistro* days, not quite with sawdust on the floor but quiet, apart from a fizzing fire, and with an assortment of ales with unlikely names like *Red Gander* and *Winter Mist*. I strode to the bar with relief, removing my rucksack whilst ordering the latter ale – it seemed to suit both the mood of the district and the inclement weather, and I was pleasantly surprised to find the barman smiling as he served me. In an arch manner, he asked me if I had been to see the lighthouse.

"Why, yes I have. How do you know? Is it a Yorkshire knack to read minds?"

"Now't else to see round here. You will have heard all about it of course...?"

"I can see that it is out of use, is there a story behind that? Stories are my stock-in-trade."

"Aye, there's a story." He glanced towards the fireplace. "I have some barrels to change; then, if you've still a mind, I'll settle your curiosity. It'll not be throng tonight."

I nodded and raised my glass, and he wandered towards the cellar door while I looked around for a comfortable seat. Being the only patron, I had the fairest of choices, and I well liked the look of a high-back chair in a dark corner near the fire where the shadows flickered in and out in a lively fashion. It was only when I got closer and my eyes adjusted to the gloom that I noticed the man. He leaned forward as if he had detached himself from the fabric of the chair opposite

11

mine.

"You American?"

"Yes sir, I am."

"I'm not keen on Americans."

This was more like the type of welcome I was familiar with, and so, not taken aback, I sat and said that I was sorry to hear that and continued in a friendly manner.

"Well, I'm guessing you are a local man, so I'm pleased to meet you at any rate. The landlord has promised to give me a little of the local history."

"If you mean the lighthouse, there's only one man to speak with" and he lifted his chin. "I was the last keeper at Spirren Head."

This was the kind of *horse's mouth* information that I adored, and I adjured him to continue, the while pulling out a notebook that had seen better days but was, at that moment, filled with the precious observances of my itinerancy.

He nodded at the notebook. "You can write this down... *I killed my wife.*"

I guess you could say that this was not quite what I expected to hear, but he continued unconcerned and said again, "Write it down, man."

I studied his face, and though his eyes had a stagnant look about them, I somehow did not disbelieve him. His face had gathered together over the years into a middle-aged rigidity of stoicism; it was not a cruel face – but there was about the lips a suggestion that this could be a hard man, and I did not doubt that, whether by accident or with aforethought, it was entirely possible. I wrote, *A man killed his wife,* and he nodded when he saw what I had written.

"I didn't hate her. 'Eck, I loved her. But I couldn't let her go, not after all those years."

I have learned that silence is the writer's tool when someone is either confessing or speaking from the heart; so, though I was taken aback, I kept my head down and scribbled as he spoke.

"My wife's name were Isolda. It's Welsh, meaning *fair.* And she were. Edward, Eddy as is, and Isolda. We grew up in Killensea where there's now't to do but cling to the things that give you pleasure and hope and that were each other. As young tykes, we were content well enough, and we sort of fell into marriage; to me it seemed natural, but as we got older...I were always afraid that she wanted more." He nodded several times.

"We both loved the sea, and when the keeper's job came up, we took it; we both regretted it. I could see from the moment we moved in how restless she were. She were still affectionate and always swore she loved me, but I knew well she were bored and unhappy, and in my frustration, I became spiteful. I'll admit that." He paused. "And then *he* came along."

I looked up. I guess I could see somewhat where this was leading, and I wondered how many times this had played out in the course of human life, with all its frailties and jealousies.

"He were American too." He leaned over and looked closely at my face; I was starting to feel uncomfortable when he sat back and continued.

"It takes at least three keepers to run a lighthouse, did you know that?"

"I didn't realise that, no."

"Aye, we struggled along for months with only the wind and the sea for company when I was told that they'd found another keeper at last. It's usual for another family to come in, but a job like that is hard to fill. My chest hurt when I saw how she looked at him, though he were pleasant enough and didn't seem to notice. Adam was a traveller, and I knew he wouldn't stick to a job such as ours for long. But he was young and adventurous, and if her head needed turning even more, he were the one to do it. I didn't believe half his tales but she did. She imagined all that she had missed, and she were right of course."

He looked down at his empty glass, and I glanced round at the bar with a view to offering him a drink. In my fascination, I had not noticed but the pub had filled somewhat despite the landlord's expectation. Before I could speak, however, he continued, and his words were heavy, whether loaded with guilt or sorrow I could not say. "He stayed longer than I thought or wanted and made himself quite at home in the settlement while we lived inside. And every day I were looking for a sign of anything but a friendship between them. I saw nothing, but still I felt pieces of her slipping away from me while I boiled inside." He paused. "Then I saw it, just a touch of the hand but it were enough..."

The flames made his eyes dance, and I began to see what jealousy

13

might do to a man, however decent they might once have been.

"I had a quiet word with him, I told him I wanted him gone that night. He said nothing but looked at me as if I were cracked, and that made the blood boil in my veins... that evening I brought Isolda here to this pub. It were busy just like it is now, and we sat here in these very seats. I told her that Adam was going away, would be gone by the time we returned."

He rubbed a hand across his face which had begun to look strained and with a certain wildness ebbing and flowing across it, as if taking on the features of that tempestuous sea he had guarded against.

"As soon as I told her, I knew I had been right to get rid. I'm not saying anything happened, but she had been unfaithful in spirit if not in the flesh; I'm not sure which is worse. I've a mind it wasn't even Adam but all that he represented that brought her discontentment to the fore; she got up with her hand over her mouth and sat in that chair over there in the corner, staring at me... then she ran to the door, hoping to see him one more time, I'm thinking."

I looked around at the now crowded pub and saw another high-back chair opposite where there now sat a pretty, yet pallid-faced and worn woman with dark hair, ill-defined against the backdrop, looking at her hands folded on the table.

"Where that lady is sitting?"

He sat stock still and stared into the uneven light.

"Where, man, where?" he lowered his voice, and I could hardly hear him above the stirred-up chatter of the locals.

"Why, there sir, right there."

He leaned towards me, almost as if for comfort, but looked hard over my shoulder, his eyes widening.

"What is she doing?" he whispered into my ear.

I glanced around in embarrassment. "She... she is looking at us..." and I felt coldness at the back of my neck as I said this, despite the heat of the fire.

"Is she by God?" he whispered again.

"It's alright, sir, she is leaving."

"IS SHE BY GOD?!!!" he roared and leapt to his feet.

I could not help but leap to my feet also and sent my chair crashing backwards in shock. With a rush to the door, Eddy was gone whilst the solid Yorkshire patrons were silenced; I guess that I reinforced

14

their belief that strangers among them were not a thing to be encouraged. I kept my head down and hurriedly followed; do not ask me why, for I am unable to provide an answer unless it be that my appetite for the macabre, for truth and resolution, have always compelled me in that way.

A north-easterly wind had picked up and chilled the winter evening yet more with its vigour and the moon had risen, low yet large and round, and by its light I could see two figures in shadowed profile ahead. The one hurried with a woman's bearing, one hand now holding a shawl that kept her long, dark hair in place, whilst the man was in all furious urgency following but still several dozen paces behind.

Do you know, try as I might to keep them in view, each time I looked they were further away, scurrying in fear and anger along the wind-blown spit until they were diminutive figures, and I beat my way through the spray that flew at me from the greasy rocks in a bid to keep them in sight.

I was aware that the tide was seeping across the narrowest part of the spit, threatening to cut me adrift from the mainland, and I was ready to turn back when something occurred that set the hackles on my neck rising. The lighthouse beam came on! It slashed through the night sky, and the surrounding darkness withdrew before it; it was a solid spear of light that may once have saved souls but to me was now just a beacon that drew me towards it in awful fascination.

I finally came near it, wet, shaking with cold and a kind of apprehension, and I made out the figure of the woman leaving the settlement's nearest abode. To me, it seemed as though she had both her hands to her head as if tearing her hair, and I guess the moaning could have been the wind or that of a woman who had lost something that she never really had; she ran into the lighthouse, and the man called Eddy followed her deliberately and slowly.

I do not know what I expected or even why I was there, but I stood, sodden, frozen, while the wind churned white sprays into my eyes and whipped and eddied around me, locking me there, the lighthouse in front and the open door of the settlement behind; I slowly raised my head and could imagine one figure flying in circular haste to the pinnacle of that tower whilst the other followed with a measured tread, whether to harm or entreat I do not know.

There are some things I will never forget. Two figures appeared,

15

swaying, locked together, crashing against the summit rails with a stream of light surrounding them, no longer sharp and straight but vaporous and clinging. If anything, the woman fought the harder, and her hands and arms beat down repeatedly while the man gripped her, it seemed desperately, until, with a cry, the woman fell – a black shape tore downwards and was dashed on the sea-hewn rocks before me.

I wanted to scream; I remember that. I wanted to scream, but the whole of me was locked in a kind of frozen terror that would not release me from its hold. Only when I forced myself to look away from that twisted form and looked upwards to see Eddy pointing a finger at me could I speak, and it was to whisper to myself repeatedly "oh Christ, oh Christ, oh Christ…" and when I saw Eddy mouth "YOU!" I ran.

I'm not ashamed to say that I ran, even though I was not exactly sure of what I had seen. I ran because Eddy had pointed at me, and his eyes were red. Mostly, I ran because Eddy did not like Americans; he had told me so himself.

I slipped and slid and stumbled my way along that spit and waded through the incoming tide with the lights of *The Wayfarer* signalling safety and a harbour within which to save myself and my sanity, perhaps. When I, at last, reeled through the door, it was into a deserted pub, and the landlord stood there in sane mundanity wiping glasses behind the bar.

He looked at me in astonishment." Good God man, what's happened to you?!"

"Give me something stronger than *Winter Mist,* and I'll tell you."

He quickly drew me a double measure of Scotch, which had me coughing, and we sat (I insisted that it was not in that corner by the fire), and when I had finished and had begun to think straight, I said we should call the police. He looked at me hard and said –

"I don't think so… Eddy has been dead these last eight years."

I kept silent.

"Killed his wife, threw her from the top of the lighthouse, but not before she stabbed him first."

"But you must have seen him! And everybody else too!"

"Not been a soul in all night." He gave a bleak laugh. "Unless you count Eddy's, of course."

"What happened to Adam, for God's sake?"

16

He rubbed his chin. "Well, some say he just upped and left, and others that Eddy lost his temper with him... no one has seen him since."

"Can you believe what I say?"

He raised his eyebrows in that slow, Yorkshire way and said –

"Looking at you, man, no one would doubt it."

So, there you have it. That good landlord bid me stay overnight and a few more days on top, free and gratis; I'll never think badly of a Yorkshireman again, unless he happens to be a lighthouse keeper.

For myself, why, I am finding Boston, Massachusetts, USA, good and honest and safe, which is how I like things now, though I sometimes lie in my bed and wonder with awfulness, and not a little pity, about those two souls grappling on the edge of eternity *for* eternity... and I consider that, though I am a proud American, that night on the Head was the one occasion I did *not* want to be such, no sir.

As for my friends, well, I think they may well have laughed and shaken their heads at my tale were it not for the fact that I returned with my hair sheer white. In consequence, and in deference to me I guess, I have heard none of them call England quaint anymore.

THE APPLICANT

Ya cain't... ya cain't ride a horse?! Well now, how you gonna be a sheriff without a horse? This ain't quite the Wild West I know, but still...

Oh, you have your own means of transport, eh? Well, sure nuff, if you say so.

Say, how'd you know there was a sheriff's vacancy anyhow? I only just put up that there sign not more than a gnat's tea time ago.

Ya got what? Good comoonications where ya come from? And where is that 'zactly? Let me write that down. T-R-A-N-S... say, that near Pennsylvania State? No? Never heerd of it.

Well now, ya done any sheriffin' before? No? Well, you ain't 'zactly selling yourself to me, feller, I gotta say. This is a man's job. You gotta keep control, you gotta have what I call a persona.

You got one of those? Yeah? They're right skeered of you in your hometown, are they? Well, I cain't 'zactly see why, you don't look any great shakes. That there cape for example – kinda dandified, ain't it? No call for it in a sheriff, unless you are goin' to the the-ay- tre. And while I'm at it, black ain't a great colour in a hot clime like this. Black suit and cape gonna eat up that sun and melt you down during the day.

What's that you say? You don't go out in the sun. Well now, when *are* you goin' to do your sheriffin'? Midnight?! Heh, heh! Now, don't be smart with me, son. I know there are a lot of ruffians in cahoots late at night causin' trouble, but I need me a full-time sheriff.

Ya carry a gun? No? Well, if you ain't the damndest pro-spective sheriff I ever come across! What you gonna do, bare your teeth at them? Whoa, feller! They sure are some teeth, I gotta say! Still, a Colt .45 would stop you in your tracks. I admire your backbone, son. You're either young and naïve or just plumb crazy.

Not young? Well, how old are you? You cain't be more 'un thirty, thirty-five... hunnerd and twenty-four?! Heh, heh! An officer of the law's gotta have a sense of humor – I like that! You might do at that. You're growing on me, feller, I'm gonna take a chance on you.

Let me tell you a little about the place. You got Belle's saloon 'cross the way, the Oppenheimer bank, couple-a grocery stores, Calhoun's Steak House on the corner... Whoa! Sit down, son. You come over all faint and pale, even paler than you was before – and that's saying some.

Fair enough, feller. I won't mention steaks again, though mysel' I like an old-fashioned garlic sauce with mi... say, if you keep coming all over unnecessary like that, you ain't gonna be worth a dime!

What are the *girls* like hereabouts? Well, that's not the kinda question a gent should be askin', but if you must know, this here town is pretty respectable – mostly married ladies, and those that ain't are working their trade over at Belle's.

Virgins? Now look here, feller. You need to wash your mouth out. What you asking 'bout virgins for? Yeah 'course, this is Virginia, but I'm guessing there ain't a virgin in the whole state!

Oh, you don't want the job now? Dammit, I'm thinkin' you been wasting my time, feller! What's your name anyhow? D-R-A-C... what kinda name's that? Git outta here! And, don't bother applying in the next state neither. West Virginia plumb run right out of virgins too!

A GOOD RUSSIAN

At a long, six-paned window, in an empty room overlooking Red Square, two men stood. If their conversation had a conspiratorial air to it, this is nothing to be surprised at in these corridors of power – such conversations are historically, albeit surreptitiously, commonplace. Life, death, peace, war – no lesser topics would suffice in these times, and inside the Kremlin, whose ramparts look down from Borovitsky Hill onto the colourful and spectacular domes of St. Basils Cathedral, these topics were uppermost in their minds.

The old general, grizzled with short cropped hair, his uniform immaculate and stretched tightly across his still powerful broad shoulders and chest, took drags from a small cigar and listened distractedly to his companion. His eyes never left the massive brick-made Red Square, the place now scattered with tourists, where the military superpower of the Soviet Union parades its might – in his eyes, not often enough.

"So, Comrade General, do I read you aright now? You and I are of the same mind?"

The taller and younger of the two, sallow faced with dark swept-back hair, spoke in hushed tones – as was wise. There was an innate arrogance in his manner, which displayed itself in his seeming indifference, but even he, though his grey eyes were cool, could not quite conceal his eagerness to hear the answer he desired. He also knew that this veteran must be treated with respect, for without him, his plans would come to naught.

General Bershov turned slowly from the window and, equally slowly, regarded the young man in his crisp white shirt, tailored navy suit – which is suspiciously Savile Row, he thought – and black brogues – a legacy, no doubt, of his time as a consul in London. He found the attire ridiculous and unsuited to a member of the Central Committee, even one as ambitious as Vikhrov. But times were changing, and with a shrug and sardonic smile, he remarked, "You and I, Comrade Vikhrov, are certainly not of the same mind... however... we do have, let us say, certain common interests."

20

Vikhrov was not annoyed at the general's response. Though disdainfully given, it was what he wanted to hear.

"Do you go to see him now?"

"I do."

There was little left to say, and more, if there were, it would be unsafe to say it; all that needed to be said had been agreed upon via trusted intermediaries in dark-lit hotel rooms, safe houses (as safe as they could be in these turbulent times), and damp park benches. Such intermediaries rarely looked each other in the eye and spoke almost unbelievingly, as if they could hardly grasp the enormity of the conspiracy they were planning. Just once before had the general met Vikhrov face to face and alone. If he were to trust this man, he wished to see what he was made of: he found that he was impressed with his efficiency, although not his moral compass.

Notwithstanding the fact that Vikhrov's raw ambition to secure a seat on the Politburo (and who knows, perhaps, thence to the General Secretaryship) sat uneasily with the general, he too knew that a reluctant alliance was necessary. The general saw himself as the saviour of the historic, although now occasionally inglorious, union of states that bestrode an ever-more unstable world, and he was willing to put aside his distaste and impatience with political intrigue for the sake of that. It was discipline and military might that kept the Soviet and thence Russia, his homeland, safe; of that, he was never more certain.

On these things, he pondered as he walked steadily along the corridors of the senate building. Although it was still impressive, he unconsciously compared them to the glories of the Grand Kremlin Palace and its interconnected buildings. In his eyes, it was yet another metaphor for the manner in which past glories were being replaced by the president's vision of a practical Soviet, with greater openness, freedoms, and the *perestroika* required to form a different kind of global influence.

The general sighed inwardly. How best to put this to the president? And if he did not see reason, would he really pursue a *coup d'état* with Vikhrov against the supreme head of the Soviet? What if it were to fail then? What would happen to Svetlana, his beloved Svetlana, whose youth and yellow-haired beauty had bewitched him these past few

21

months? Reaching the president's outer offices, he shook that old head of his and straightened once more the shoulders that had carried more than their fair share of war- imposed responsibility and now bore an even heavier political one. He was ushered in to face the man who he was prepared to betray, if need be. Comrade President stood by the window with his back to the room; the irony was not lost on Bershov that the president regarded the very same vista that he himself had viewed only a few minutes before. The room was silent, and the general waited patiently. Suddenly, the president turned as though he'd just realised he was not alone.

"Ah, Comrade General! Welcome, welcome. Sit down, please." He motioned towards the stiff-backed chair facing a large mahogany desk behind which he himself sat down; despite his stoutness, he moved quickly, quietly and with poise. When the general looked at his face, he recognised again the surprisingly kind eyes, which were benign behind gold-rimmed spectacles. He also knew, however, that behind those eyes there was a mind prepared to be ruthless when needed.

The general cleared his throat. He had rehearsed the words that he wanted to say – the words that would convey his conviction that the road the president had chosen, this *glasnost,* would inevitably lead to the diminution – no, the ruin – of the greatness, the security, the union and thence the country he held dear. He took a breath, ready to expound his passionate argument, his plea for restraint and the status quo.

The president held up his right hand. "Please, Comrade General, please. There is no need." He slowly opened a drawer with his left hand, withdrew a buff folder and placed it upon the desk. It was plain and simple but was no less intimidating because it was stamped in red ink with "classified".

"General… General Bershov… let me say this – you have served your country well. Who does not know that? Your reputation for integrity and bravery is not just a matter of public record, but it is also written in the hearts of those who have followed you into conflict many times and would gladly do so again." He looked down at the folder and shook his head – rather sadly, it appeared to Bershov. "It is this affection and loyalty that make things difficult for me. My admiration for you is a genuine one, and in many ways, you and I believe in the same things, at least all of the important things – honour, principle, the greatness and security of the union and, most of all, our beloved Russia. But thereafter, we differ… times are changing, the world is changing, and we must change too. We cannot hold onto the past."

The president's fleshy yet elegant fingers opened the folder. With only a slight start, the general recognised Vikhrov's features in several photographs. The navy-blue suit, evidently a favourite of his, appeared often, and the general could not help thinking how incongruous it looked in comparison with the drab greyness of the compatriots who appeared in conversation with him.

Dryly, the president commented, "Comrade Vikhrov, as we speak, is being escorted to a place where he will have plenty of time to reflect upon certain unwise ambitions." Again, he raised his hand. "Please, do not mistake me, General. All will be fair and above board. There must, and will, be open justice in the new Soviet." He softly added, "Yet, sometimes, the old methods may still be the best."

"For yourself," he continued, "it is certainly a quandary. There are no words for what you planned other than subversion and treason… and yet… and yet… you are a man, like myself, of principle, and you did what you did, unlike Vikhrov, not for your own gain." He paused. "What actions can now be taken?" He frowned, more in puzzlement than in anger.

Bershov realised that he had not said a word yet, although he knew any eloquence that an old general could muster would have made no difference at all. Besides, with a swiftness that had taken him by surprise, he also gathered that the opportunity for persuasion had passed. A single word was all that he could force through his lips.

"How?"

The president pressed a concealed button, and within a moment, the door through which Bershov had recently entered quietly opened. When he turned, he was not entirely surprised to see her smooth-complexioned face. Her eyes, although colder than they were last evening when he had looked into them, were still deep and liquid blue. With her lightly glossed full lips, she had whispered breathy, heady words to a lonely man. Her yellow hair still shone, though it was pulled straight now and tied tightly behind her ears, making them look larger than usual. "All the better for listening with," he thought wryly.

He stood and walked past Svetlana without a glance towards the two guards who waited patiently behind her. The president nodded to them, and they deferentially closed around Bershov and escorted him out of the office.

The president sighed and muttered softly to himself, "Yes, yes, the old ways are sometimes the best," and shook his head. He rose and stood before Svetlana, and looking into that cold wonderful face, he was tempted to kiss her himself. But being *a man of principle*, as he often told himself and others, he thought of his wife and dismissed her until she was needed again.

THE LADY IN THE ROOM

When someone steps into my office, it means one of two things – a pay check or trouble. If it's a broad, it's usually just the latter; they rely real heavy on the "dame-in-distress" gambit, and with those who got noble feelings, it works just dandy. Except I don't. I got to earn a living, don't I?

With a guy, well yeah, there are some cheapskates out there, and a lot of them end up here, or places much like it, but with them I can play hardball a little and squeeze their pips; they all got troubles for which I occasionally find solutions. If I don't, they pay anyway. I don't work for nothing.

You can see I ain't no Marlowe; that guy don't do us dicks no favors. You read about him and he's a principled guy and he's set that particular bar high – too bad. It's just a little higher than I care to jump over. Sure, I got principles too, but as some hick once said, "if you don't like them, I got others". Okay, he plays chess and he's kind of smart; so, what? On those counts I match him. But the similarities end there bud, I can tell you that.

On one hot, unmoving Manhattan day, when the street sounds were forced to fight their way to the second floor, I looked up from nothing and watched a heavy silhouette mark time outside my door. I could tell its owner was looking real carefully at the graven lettering on the frosted glass, *Aaron Baum, Private Investigator*, and he was none too sure he wanted any further introductions. I leaned back and waited; I knew he would knock eventually. They always do.

His knock was firm enough, brusque even, and he strode in without waiting for permission. I recognised him straightaway; he was both expensive and expansive, his suit being of the tailor-made kind, the pinstripe making my eyes itch while he filled the room with a bulk I ain't seen since Big Joe Turner played the *Café Society* club. Don't get me wrong, in this room if you swung two cats by the tail, they might just clear the walls, but his size was the intimidating kind, and I guess intimidating others is just what he had been doing all his life – you don't get to be a big player in this city without a little coercion.

25

I pushed back my chair but didn't stand.

"Take a pew, Mr. Marino."

If knowing his name was supposed to impress him, it didn't. He looked around at the fly-spotted walls.

"Nice place you have here," he sneered impassively.

"Thank you… if you want to help me decorate sometime, be my guest."

He narrowed his eyes and sat down.

"Funny guy, huh?"

"Sure, it's the only entertainment around here."

We sat in silence. Something told me he wasn't too impressed with my attitude, and in the interest of moving things forward, I asked what I could do to help a rich and powerful guy such as himself. I guess he took that as a compliment, as he grinned like a wolf and said he'd come right to the point.

He reached inside his jacket, stretching his waistcoat taut like the skin on a hog, and pulled out a small, neat photograph. Even upside down, I could see it was of a lady with class, her hair and eyebrows were black and as glossy as the paper and when I took the photo, equally dark eyes looked into mine; I didn't like the hunted look in them or the fragile tilt of the chin, and I tossed it onto the desk. My voice got a little frostier.

"Missing, huh?"

He raised an eyebrow. "Never for long."

"You mean she comes running back to her loving husband?". I decided to sneer too; it was that kind of an afternoon.

"I mean I find her…" He narrowed his eyes a little, enough to give me the willies and make me angry.

"Oh, I see… You slap her around a little, huh?"

He flushed and got angry.

"What I do in the privacy of my own home has nothing to do with you. You're a lousy dick earning lousy peanuts in a lousy profession." The way he said it, it was a matter of fact.

I sighed. "What are you doing here, Mr. Marino?"

He quietened down a little. "I heard you were good."

"I thought I was lousy?"

"Yeah, well, you got me angry… it doesn't do well to get me

26

angry, Mr. Baum."

I raised both my eyebrows and said, "I'm guessing your wife has found that out" and, before he could hit the desk, "I'll find her for you, Mr. Marino."

"Well now, that's sensible, yes indeed it is" He nodded and licked his lips like one of those cats would look if it struck lucky for some cream.

"I don't come cheap."

He looked around the room as if he couldn't believe his ears. I swear to God, if he had sneered again, I would have put a hard, cold fist deep into his soft, red face. Instead, he asked what my daily charge would be.

"Forty dollars a day plus expenses."

He shrugged and bragged, "That sounds cheap to me."

"In that case Mr. Marino, let's make it fifty dollars a day, a week in advance. For ease of calculation and to get the ball rolling, I'll take a check, made to cash, for four hundred dollars."

He looked as though the cream he might have swallowed earlier had been soured by a lemon, but pride made him take out a pocket book, veneered in crocodile leather, and a pen that would have cost half of my fee.

He threw the check across the desk. I looked at it and reassured him it was a good deal. "You must spend more than this on a couple of nights at the *Grand Plaza* with your lady friends."

I smiled a little smugly while he angrily told me he was a respectable businessman, and that any accusations of that kind were likely to land me without a business and quite possibly with no legs worth standing on.

I got up and crossed the room on my legs while I could still walk on them and opened the door. There were individual sounds, workman-like and full of activity, fluttering like butterfly wings from every one of the offices behind the tawdry brown doors; those doors and the stains on the landing carpet reminded me of how far I hadn't come up in the world.

"Goodbye, Mr. Marino. You'll be hearing from me."

I watched as he walked along the corridor, trying not to touch the walls and determined not to look back. He couldn't resist it, and before he took off down the stairs, gave me one last look of disgust and reproof;

27

he managed to fit in one of warning at the same time.

I closed the door and then sat at my desk watching a fly crawl on the opposite wall for 10 minutes. I thought hard a little too. When I felt certain he was gone, I opened a drawer and pulled out an ochre folder, the newest thing I owned, and put the photo of the hunted lady on top of several other pictures.

The sun was low and red, the light seeping through the blinds when I finally got up to leave. I locked the door, purely to make myself feel like I had something worth stealing, and made my way out into the Manhattan evening.

The breeze that had sprung up took a welcome edge off my thoughts, and when the city lights began to glow like cigarette ends, I felt like picking up the pace home. I carried the folder and patted the check inside my jacket pocket; my smile was slanted; I just knew it.

The subway from Broadway and 157th was full of workers, with the possibility that at least some of them were keen to get home to their wives, and I disembarked at 137th. I ain't sentimental, but for once I hesitated, and instead of heading for LaSalle Street, I took a long, thoughtful detour onto Old Broadway and stood for a while in front of the synagogue, the only one in either Manhattanville or Harlem, and thought of my *ima,* long gone; she always told me that nothing good would come from a job that involved poking my *klutz* nose into somebody else's business. I slanted my smile again and traced my steps home.

My office might be an idling point for the occasional discerning fly, with a mote or more of dust to make it feel comfortable, but I take pride in my apartment; it's kind of elegant in an understated, partial art deco way. When I turned the key and opened the door, there, by the muted table light, Mrs. Marino was sitting on my olive, high– backed two–seater, turning over a chess piece in her hands. She stood up with a nervous smile, but the brittle look of a week ago had gone, and the bruises under those intense black eyes had faded, such that she merely looked as though she hadn't slept so good for a night or two.

"Mr. Baum, you are late tonight, I was getting worried about you." I think she meant it too, and she said it in a voice that was as smooth as a *grasshopper* cocktail; it made me feel like having a drink myself, and I helped myself to a bourbon on the rocks and offered the same to her. She shook her head slightly and asked –

"Did he... did he come today?"

Her right hand was fluttering nervously at her porcelain neck, while the left clutched the chess piece tightly, such that her knuckles whitened; I couldn't see what the piece was. It kind of occurred to me that if it was a pawn, it wouldn't have been out of place – she was as defenseless as one against her husband and a chess–board city full of bribed, corrupt rooks and crooks.

I asked her to sit down and sipped my bourbon.

"Yeah, guys like him always come to guys like me when they got nowhere else to go. We didn't hit it off so good."

I felt kind of satisfied about that, and opening the folder, I placed the photos on the wood bean coffee table next to my chess set. Apart from the one of herself, all of the others were of her husband and a variety of broads entering and leaving the *Grand Plaza*. Pride of place, courtesy of a bell-hop pal of mine and thirty bucks, was one of the intimate kind. She averted her eyes, and I felt kind of dirty but knew that these photos were her escape route, and I told her so.

I went kind of gentle on her and told her softly that he wouldn't want the rags to get hold of those, that the threat would be enough for him to stop chasing her around. She looked doubtful, but I knew his kind well. I took out the check for four hundred dollars and handed it to her and told her to cash it first thing in the morning. I threw in an extra fifty bucks in ten-dollar bills of my own.

She stood up and faced me square; I liked the way she looked at me, and I liked the way she didn't look hunted any more.

"I...I don't know how to thank you. I will always remember your kindness." She opened her hand. "What piece is this, Mr. Baum?" The mahogany piece was stark against the whiteness of her palm.

"That's called a knight, Mrs. Marino."

"Ah..." She touched my cheek. "Sir Galahad," she said, smiling and then turned towards the bedroom. "Goodnight, Mr. Baum."

I took the spare bedding and laid them out for a final night on a couch that was a size too small and gave a silent whistle and an *Oy Vey* as she closed the door.

I guess I'm nobler than I thought, *Ima. Shalom.*

A POINT OF VIEW

Dad was brilliant today. When my friends (no girls!) arrived for my 8th birthday party, he said hello to all of them and smiled a lot, and then took their coats upstairs to hang up; when he got back he did some magic tricks for us.

Most of us pretended not to notice when he put that card in his pocket. Charlie Higgs was all for shouting it out loud until I gave him a Chinese burn and got Porky Allen to sit on him. Dad says it's not politically correct – whatever that is – to call someone a name like that. Of course, Porky doesn't know we call him that; we're not stupid – he'd kill us!

Mum brought the food in and we followed Porky's lead and dug into the cakes. The sandwiches were left untouched; I could see Mum looking a bit glum, so I nibbled at a cheese sandwich until she wasn't looking, then shoved it behind the sofa.

We went into the garden where Dad had organised some games, but the best bit was when Dad tried to show how good he was at football. He was crap. We laughed our heads off! But he did do a fantastic header from a cross by Charlie that went straight past Porky who was in goal – which takes a lot of skill as Porky fills most of it up.

I think Dad enjoyed the party even more than I did!

*

Harold was feeling nervous. The bell rang; and when he opened the door a gang of kids swept in – he couldn't see how many, but they damn near knocked him over. While they rushed past him and threw their coats at him, he made himself smile. He took the coats upstairs and stood there uncertainly; then he thought, *sod it,* and flung the coats on the bed.

He was apprehensive about the little magic display that he had been working on, but after the event he was confident that it had gone well (so easy to fool these kids!). He had an uneasy suspicion that the little bugger (what was his name – Charlie?) had spotted something, but he felt that had got away with it. The food went down well, at least the cakes did; he knew they wouldn't eat the sandwiches, even the chubby lad didn't want them!

They were sods in the garden. It was a waste of time organising games; all they wanted to do was play football. Harold didn't mind that too much, he thought he could show them a thing or two, and things were going fine until that bloody Charlie smashed the ball into his face. He had a notion it was deliberate – Christ it hurt! He was still rubbing his face when the lot of them buggered off. Thank God!

ASSASSIN'S VACATION

The assassin's weapon of choice depends entirely on his preference and the circumstance under which he is to operate.

Andrapov was patriotic enough to have chosen a Russian-made VSS sniper rifle with a silencer, specially modified to be broken down and reassembled quickly. He had used it before. It was a silent killer, like himself. It suited him, and he felt comfortable in its company.

He was a cold fish with a face that was darkly cruel but not unhandsome. He had learned to his advantage that many women had a preference for his kind of latent danger; they could see it in the blue-grey eyes that were generally indifferent until anger excited them with an intense red.

He could be charming when he needed to be... and cruel... but only in the line of business. It was an asset much admired by his superiors. That is why he was here, on the third floor of a grey tenement in Navarra, assembling the VSS. And that is also why the body of the middle-aged landlady lay neatly strangled on the dishevelled bed in the corner.

He had chosen his position well. Any of the balconies on the numerous private tenements would have provided a covering darkness suited to his purpose; he need only sit back in the sultry gloom. This room, however, had the advantage of overlooking the bend between Mercaderes and Estafeta, an enviable position during the Festival of San Firmín when the crowds of the notorious Pamplona Bull Run, *El Encierro*, would surge past this now-deadly spot – his mark in sight and within 200 metres.

He perceived no irony in the fact that this place was known as Dead Man's Corner. His only feeling was slight contempt at the knowledge that an enemy counterpart would choose to holiday at all. He considered that his target must be a fool after all, despite his reputation. He was surely aware that spies and assassins never relax, are never on holiday, and are always, *always*, on guard. His respect for him diminished even as he loaded a single 9 mm bullet – he would only need the one.

He leaned back and listened in the sudden silence. There was a barely audible hum as the runners chorused the first chant to San Firmín, which gained in volume such that on the fifth chant, the roaring bulls were released. He could not see them yet, but he knew that the *pastores* would be driving the angry animals charging along the narrow road to the bull ring half a mile away.

The clamour of the bystanders and the excited and, yes, frightened, runners increased, and uncoordinated bellows preceded both animals and humans who swept into sight. The full run would take 3 minutes, and he was calm – he had never yet missed. He settled the VSS snugly on his right shoulder and poised his left eye along the line of telescopic sight.

Yasneyev had informed him that the target would neither be wearing the traditional red sash, white pants and shirt, nor the red *panuelico* neck scarf. He had instead chosen green and gold – an arrogance that would mark him out even in such a crowd. And that, in Andrapov's eyes, was yet another failing.

He knew a man such as he would be at the fore, and as the bellowing madness surged into view, his finger curled on the trigger. There! There he was... a torso of white crossed with a waist of green and gold. His finger tightened... and held. Where was his green and gold scarf?

From the corner of his eye, along the drab "off white" wall of the room, he saw a red laser dot dart down over the cracks to mark him for death.

He remained still, only his eyes moved and he saw across the street, one floor above his own, in an equally drab tenement, at an equally propitious balcony, a glimpse of green and gold. Andrapov gave a single nod in acknowledgment before a dark hole appeared with a thump between his eyes.

The man in the green and gold scarf turned coolly and moved swiftly back into the darkness.

Andrapov was right – spies and assassins never holiday.

TWO FINGERS OF RYE

A hot wind had chased him all the way down from Colorado into New Mexico, and the air had not cooled even after he had crossed the Pecos, that wild tributary running almost a thousand miles before spilling into the mouth of the mighty Rio Grande in Texas.

His horse rode drudgingly, head down like himself, both pale with the dirt of the trail. His Stetson was pulled low, and the grimed collar of his long canvas duster was wrapped tightly about his ears – yet still he could hear the wind whip through the mesquite plants. As hard as his nature and circumstances had made him, he was a weary man, but it was not the travelling that had made him this way.

He had ridden a once proud and scornful palomino throughout the western states for more years than he cared to remember, unafraid to be seen, his reputation with a gun preceding him like the shadow of a raven. Like as not, the granite of his face and the heated look in his sun-shot eyes precluded confrontation with all but the harshest and hardiest of men; this at a time when many men were of this ilk. Yet, just as likely, there was always someone, vainglorious and anxious to prove himself in the only way they knew how, who was willing to risk a kind of reputational death at his hands.

Of course, the law had something to say; if a man dies, there is always reason and cause, though neither necessarily just. The law had little interest in understanding that he was not a *natural born killer*. Though others of his breed hired their guns, that had not been his way, and though he had ridden with the James-Youngers for a brief headstrong period, he was neither, instinctively, a thief. He needed to eat like any man, but the hunger that he had originally felt in his hot-headed youth had been only the desire to prove he was the best, the fastest with a gun.

Yet when he eventually came out of Yuma Penitentiary, something inside him had altered. He tried but could not avoid confrontation; death was invariably the outcome, and he felt a bitterness that it should always be this way, and he sought a kind of shuffling anonymity.

The small town grew out of a shroud of dust and revealed its face to be somewhat untypical of the towns west of the Pecos, which were an invariable amalgam, even in the daylight hours, of clamour and lawlessness. He passed a tiny and pretty clapboard house on the outskirt. As he did so, the wind, in an instance, plumbed like a stone, and the silence struck him like a panhandler's shovel. The dust blanketed the ground, and he was able to stop at last, wipe the chafing grit from his eyes, and look down a long, narrow street lined with the normal miscellany of 1870's old west shops, a bank, and a saloon.

It had long been his custom to make the saloon his first place of call in a new town. Two fingers of rye whiskey seemed to briefly settle the devil in his mind; that devil was once manifest in a heated itch to draw his Smith and Wesson Model 3 at whatever he deemed provocation. Yet, more recently, it was like the irritation of a pepper vine and a trembling that would not be entirely stilled.

The saloon lay two short blocks down, with an exterior as pristine in its way as the clapboard house, leastwise as pristine as a saloon ever gets. He had yet to find one that did not reflect its clientele, which in all cases was as rough and ready as one could imagine.

He shook his head and pulled his steed up outside, looking the while at the deep black horseshoe which hung upside down above the two louvre doors – the luck running out of it – then espying a stable across the street and being the conscientious horseman that as a boy he was brought up to be, he led his horse across the way.

A cheery whistling somewhat resembling a song from the old Chisholm trail reached his ears, and he realised that this was the first person he had cognizance of since his arrival. It struck him this was the sort of quiet town he had been looking for since Yuma, and a kind of peacefulness fell upon him - a lonesome, aching feeling, unfamiliar since his Ma had begged him not to go into town some 20 years ago to kill his first man.

The stable-hand looked up from sweeping a stall with a long-handled brush, then stood erect, placing the brush aside with his left hand and bringing his right hand up to proudly stroke a moustache that hung two inches each side of a friendly mouth. He smiled as he did so and spoke.

"Aft'noon, stranger. That fine animal looks worn. Feed and water?"
The man nodded. "Be obliged."

"Here long?"

Slowly, the man, as worn as his horse, smiled and said, "I may stay awhile." He handed the reins to the hand, nodded once more, and headed back across the street to the saloon without its luck.

The stable-hand looked after him thoughtfully, this time bringing up two forefingers to pull down on both sides of his moustache. He seemed to make up his mind and hurriedly closed and bolted the stable doors, before striding quickly towards the far end of the street. Entering a saloon in a strange town is a disquieting experience for any man. For this man in particular, the disquiet had not grown less as time passed. Though his notoriety had diminished as he had hoped it would, the aura that surrounds a gunman is a cloak of menace, indistinct and imprecise yet detectable to all those attuned to the need for self-preservation.

He kept his hat on and his head down, but when he looked up to give his order to the barman, he was pleasantly surprised to find that little notice had been taken of him by those few coarse cowboys who were occupied in playing poker at one of the small round tables. He swallowed his rye at a gulp and relaxed enough to order another, a rarity. But this time, he took his glass to the safest place he could see, a table in the far corner where he sat with his back to the wall, facing the batwing doors that swung from time to time as a patron entered or left.

Placing his hat carefully to the right of the table, the better to obscure any movement of his gun hand, he heaved out a sigh, as he realised it would always be this way – his life always guarded, both consigned and confined to a self-protectionism, and a prison of his own making. The sigh was a wearisome sound, weighted down with the souls of a dozen men.

He sat and nursed his thoughts and his drink. A summer reverie came upon him, redolent with the whispers of memories that grew louder in his mind such that he could hear, and then see, his Ma scolding him as a boy, though she did it with love and a frequent smile. He saw the foals maturing as he brought them up with care to full growth on a sunlit farmstead. He heard his own laughter as he ran with them through purple sage. Yet, he heard too the sound of gunfire as he practiced daily behind the small ranch house, feeling that there was more to life than this idyllic ennui while his Ma's face grew darker as he drew his gun faster and shot with an accuracy that had to be seen to be believed.

The famous man had come to town four miles hence. He was wanted and he was deadly, and the youth knew that was his chance. He had saddled a young palomino and ridden to the town as though he was a vengeful knight, though there was nothing to personally avenge, merely to prove himself and earn himself repute. The thought now rang through his head as his voice had rung it out upon the day he returned.

"Ma, I did it, Ma! I was faster than him, Ma!!" And she had replied with a choking leadenness, "You killed a man, son," and he could not make her understand. He had eventually turned and ridden away because, in fact, he did not know himself why he had done what he had done. With a sudden self-loathing, his life was set, as full of desolation as if it were a gulch cactus that stood weathered through all the seasons, beset by change but unchanging, alone.

"Hey, Mister! I know who you are!"

For a moment, his musing was interrupted by stark reality as he heard the same challenging words that he himself had used those many years before. The youth stood less than 10 feet from him – skinny, with recalcitrant hair the colour of sun kissed hay, and intense yet distracted eyes that had not found their focus on life, still searching but not knowing what for. He recognised those eyes as the projection of something wild and untamable but with an inherent virtuousness; for a weary second, he saw that spirit as his own and prayed for a way out – for himself, the boy, and every soul that had to make a choice.

"You're wanted for killing…"

"Not in this state, son". He interrupted but kept his voice level, knowing that any inflection would likely mean the death of himself or the boy. He did not want to kill but was not quite reconciled to dying himself. Yet, as he looked steadily into the youthful eyes, he realised that more than death he feared for a lost life in front of him, whichever way this turned.

He made up his mind and did what he had not done in 20 years of conflict, and as the sheriff and the stable-hand hurried through the doors and the sheriff's concerned voice hollered an imprecation to the boy, he reached for his hat to walk away.

The sheriff would later swear honestly, by all that was holy, that it certainly *looked* as though he was going for his gun, and with a man like that, could there be any doubt?

The veteran saw that this young man was fast, perhaps faster than he himself had been at that age, but knew also with over half a lifetime of action and reaction and of "kill or be killed", that had he been prepared, he would still be the faster of the two. Perhaps it really was his unpreparedness or perhaps, he thought as he fell to the deadening blast and the all too familiar smell of cordite and the crushing jolt of pain in his chest, he was ready to give in, to relinquish that crown he had earned and wished he hadn't; perhaps, it was just his time.

These thoughts, like his survival reactions over the years, took merely an instant, but he knew as the darkness began to draw in on him that there was just time. The boy knelt over him, not feeling how he thought he would feel, the smoking gun in his hand, and the man looked with a kind of desperation into those confused eyes and with an effort, slowly shook his head. He could not speak, no words could he force to his drying tongue try though he would, so he gently laid his hand on the boy's forearm and lowered it towards the blood- flecked floor.

He heard the Sheriff speaking softly to the boy. "Joey... Joey... let's get you home to your Ma..."

And when he heard the gun fall with a delicate finality to the floor and saw Joey stand and cover his eyes with both hands, he smiled and closed his own and saw his own Ma with arms outstretched, waiting for him in the failing light.

PENNY REICHMANN

Penny Reichmann turned heads. Not literally, it wasn't her job or anything; but if male heads could swivel 360 degrees as she high stepped through the office on the way to her desk, they would have.

There were two things that prevented any blatant head swivelling. First, she was the boss – always willing to let others know it. She was the Chief Investment Officer at one of those British financial institutions, similar to many, that take the public's money and appear to gamble with it. Second, her eyes were like blue chips of ice, appropriately enough; and if other eyes met them, the temperature dropped swifter than a bear market.

Her cheekbones were so sharp, you could cut your lips on them (although they would never be allowed that close); and she was harder than the nails she would gladly use on your coffin, if you made the wrong move on her.

Once behind her desk, the slim legs that made up a good proportion of her body were hidden from view. But beneath her exquisitely cut D & G jackets, she wore titanium white blouses that occasionally slid to the side – a bonus of the non-financial kind, but welcome to viewers of, and investors in, fine art.

It was galling for both the women in the office, who envied everything about her, from her sleek, shoulder-length black hair, down to her elegant but strong feet, which were encased in Jimmy Choo's. She knew her job and she did it well; the men too, resented this, but more particularly resented her unattainability.

One afternoon, in the summer of 2007, something happened that is the stuff of legend in financial circles – Penny Reichmann smiled. No one knew why, but she was evidently in a good mood – some speculated she may have run over a cat or some such thing.

It was shy, nervy Anthony, who sat nearest to the ice maiden's cave and dealt in futures – but did not have one of his own – who was the shocked recipient of her smile. It was a cold and slightly predatory smile perhaps, but a smile all the same. Unnerved, he immediately lost £1.2 million on a trade.

The story got around and it was jokingly said that if she ever smiled again, the markets would crash.

The next time she did so was in autumn, the same year. Unfortunately, she worked for Northern Rock.

*All characters fictitious!

LIGHT AND DARK

I have often commented to myself (I value my solitude and, therefore, live alone), whilst looking out at Harley Street, observing the constant flow of genteel humanity – how little we know of our fellow man.

Two women walk by now, respectably dressed, nudging each other and looking slyly at another as she passes – what does that mean? There again… a businessman steps down from a hansom cab, pulls out his Hunter watch and looks around him guiltily – what could be occupying him?

Lightness and darkness – two sides of the same coin. Who knows which side the coin will land!

I fancy myself as something of an amateur psychologist, although a former GP, and now, a surgeon by profession; the latter is well remunerated and allows me to lease these my first-floor apartments as both offices and domestic spaces combined, which suits my purpose perfectly. I am comfortably off, and comfortable here too, in these premises.

No doubt my fellow surgeons at Guy's regard me as something of an eccentric, and so, they only converse with me when necessary; I suppose they may have some explanation for that, but I don't care for it, I have my own principles as well as my foibles. For instance, two days ago, I barely restrained myself from bodily ejecting a lady (I use the term loosely) who wished for me to terminate an unborn child.

The autumn and early winter of 1888 has seen my caseload increase considerably. By day, I consult here in my rooms and operate at Guy's; by evening, I have lately taken it upon myself to carry out charitable visits to the children at the Royal London in the East End. I do what I can, which is little enough… those poor wretches.

In my high-backed chair, I am at ease. I have my books – prime amongst them, Gray's Anatomy, and with an ounce of shag at hand, I draw on my pipe as I revisit the events of the passing days. For instance, yesterday was again a busy one; an operation with complications, apropos to a burst appendix, strained us all, and by the evening, I was half-inclined to forgo my trip to Whitechapel, but felt I

41

could not disappoint either the nurses or the children.

As I hailed a hansom, the street lights were being lit, the lighter doffing his hat as I passed, and I could feel a tightness closing in upon us; the "pea-souper" for which London is renowned, which had been lightly suffocating us by day, together with the darkening cloud-filled sky induced a sense of swirling, deepening gloom. Restlessly, I threw my Gladstone bag, replete with medical supplies and the tools of my profession, on the seat beside me and bade the coachman to swiftly take me to the Royal. The hooves clattered sharply as the coachman flicked his whip, yet even before we reached our destination, these same hooves sounded even less distinct as the dull, damp smog thickened.

I will not weary you with the details of my visit to those benighted children; suffice it to say that I was ready to fulfil my intended walk back to Harley Street, which lies an hour distant, through the streets I know well. God knows I needed that exercise to douse the fever in my thoughts.

It was as I was passing Dutfield's Yard, off Berner Street, one of those long nondescript alleys that abound in the East End of London, that I heard a cry, a woman's cry, short and stifled, only a moment long, yet resonant with terror. I could see two indistinct forms struggling in the gloom, and with a "Hi there! You!", I rushed towards them, my cane raised. In my youth, I had been considered an able boxer and stick fighter, and a few blows to the shoulders and the head were enough to make a shabbily dressed ruffian in a peaked cap take to his heels, whilst a tall woman in a black jacket and skirt stood in front of me, breathing heavily, her hands at her mouth.

I recall distinctly that she wore a posy of red roses in her lapel, set in a spray of asparagus leaves.

She spoke, "Thank you, sir, thank you!". The accent was Nordic, so when I gently asked her name, I was surprised when she replied, "Elizabeth, sir. But most calls me Liz."

She looked at my smart top coat and matching hat, and her demeanour altered into something akin to an air of coquettishness, a parody in effect.

"Can I do anyfing for you, sir?"

She lifted her skirts with both hands. I could sense her slight unease when I reached down to open my Gladstone from where I had flung it.

It took but a moment to slit her throat. Had there been no disturbance from the adjacent working men's club, I would have severed her ear and gotten straight to that work for which I was becoming notorious; as it was, I proceeded homewards briskly, but I fear the blood-lust took hold of me, and I felt that same irresistible compulsion to kill again.

God knows! God knows why! Lightness and darkness.

I left Catherine (I like to know their names) in Mitre Square. This time, I neatly disembowelled her with clinical finesse, though the rags will report it as the work of a mad man, I am sure.

In the light of morning, I now reach for a card to scribble on it a few anonymous lines at my bureau, and address it to the authorities; if I were as proficient in psychology as I aspire to be, I would understand why I am doing this. In a moment of drollery, I sign it "Saucy Jack" with a flourish, and my wit makes me smile. So very different from the epithets of "Leather Apron", the "Whitechapel Murderer" or "Ripper" as the rags and *penny dreadfuls* would have it.

Lightness and darkness. Sunshine and shadow.

In my high-backed chair, I draw on my pipe contentedly, in the certain knowledge that winter is nigh and dark nights will arrive ever earlier.

THE GREAT MAN

My daddy – he's worked in the movies for as long as I can remember, leastwise he did till he finally retired last fall, and to listen to him, you'd swear he created all those movie stars personally rather than sat behind a camera filming them.

Before you get the wrong idea, he was no hotshot director – just a workaday cameraman, but he had more than a few bags of skill and a good eye, and maybe he did play his part at that. Let's consider it: who and what we see up there on that big old screen ain't exactly real, is it? It's maybe a smattering of reality with plenty of flimflammery, justifiable in the name of entertainment, and veneered with glamour – courtesy of the director, the make-up girls, lighting techs, and a whole damn host of others, and not least the camera men. Hell, even the soundmen have a role to play, though my daddy hates to admit it. In short, those great movie stars are of human proportions, with the same blemishes and faults as the rest of us – just that it doesn't seem that way once the final cut's been made, and we crane our necks looking up *at* them and up *to* them.

Having said that, he's met them all, or so he says, and if you believe him, he was on first-name terms with the best of them; it was a regular Who's Who of Hollywood's Golden Age, and if he wasn't having a snifter with Humphrey Bogart or Errol Flynn, he was flirting with Lauren Bacall or Ava Gardner.

Now, don't ask me why they would spend such time with a humble cameraman, though he was one of the best; and don't ask me either why I would believe it – I can only say that he was my daddy and my hero, and a boy who loves his daddy is inclined to believe everything he is told. I'm surprised I could close my eyes at all after listening with them wide open with wonderment to those Tinsel Town tales of an evening when I should have been asleep. One thing I will say: Daddy had respect for those artistes of the silver screen, and though there were one or two who were rough around the edges, and some who drank to excess and forgot their lines, and *plenty* who couldn't act a damn, he'd say with familial pride that they were all *Stars* – every single one of

44

them.

The greatest and handsomest and starriest of them all, so he told me, was Mr. James McLelland – and he was a gentleman to boot, he affirmed. He always, and I mean always, said hello in a natural British way when he saw my daddy and doffed his hat, and when hats went out of fashion, tipped him a salute and a smile instead. I hadn't watched too many of his films, but I could see where Daddy was coming from – he was tall for the Forties and the Fifties, just on 6 feet, with a lean, patrician profile made for ladies to swoon over and hair so thick and wavy and dark, the camera almost made a star out of it by itself; he was kind of elegance personified, both on and off the screen. Of course, there were also those striking hazel eyes which added to his charm but his greatest asset was, as my daddy put it, that he could *"actually act by God!"*

I like to imagine Mr. McLelland partaking of regular post-shoot or pre-prandial drinks at the bar with my daddy and convivially chewing the fat with him about both the eminence and the foibles of Hollywood royalty. I only hope he did not notice when the drink began to take its toll on dear old Dad; of course, the long days of shooting were a presentable excuse, but how he kept the camera trained so perfectly over the next thirty years was a testament to something – perhaps his love for me and the need to keep a roof over our heads. Things only turned bad when his memory began to fade; I guess the booze didn't help, but that wasn't the cause, I know that now.

Now, having taken after Daddy in a way, not with the drinking but being accorded his skill with a camera and an eye for detail, it seemed inevitable that I would end up in the business in some way or the other. I did, but I was just astute enough to see that the Golden Age had come and gone, and it was with that magic box in the corner of the room, with its blinking, winking eye, the focus of every American apple-pie family, plus the lonely and the downright lazy, where the future lay – TV had arrived big time, and I hung onto its coat-tails and worked and hustled my way over the years to reach somewhere near the top of the production tree. I sold out and swapped the big screen for the small. I hated myself, and Daddy didn't like it, but he still loved me, naturally.

I was away working on one of those mediocre but lucrative productions I specialized in when I finally met the great star. The day

45

had been a long one, and though the hotel bar was noisy, buzzing with the crew who claimed their right to let their hair down after a boring day's shoot, I heard it clearly from the reception desk: "Goodnight Mr. McLelland, sir." I whipped my head around, and the elevator doors, of silver and shining brass within which the clamorous, end-of-the-day crowd was reflected, closed just a little too quickly. Of course, had I seen him I might not have recognised him – he surely must have been in his septuagenarian dotage, and would he want to be bothered by the son of a former cameraman? But he was Daddy's friend, wasn't he? I had to see him, I knew then I wouldn't be able to sleep, just like that child never could, who in his formative years was raised on tales of glamour and dreams.

It took fifty dollars and the promise of a bit part (silent) in my next production to obtain Mr. McLelland's room number from the receptionist. It was touching to see an authentic reticence on the part of the old guy behind the desk, who seemed respectful and protective of someone whom he called *"a real gent"*, and he gave me the number only when I assured him of my best intentions. I think he could sense that it was a kind of nostalgic connection to my childhood; and, though he didn't know it, my daddy's past – a past when his mind was strong and clear and not tangled and sticky with whatever it is that makes you forget and become someone others don't recognize anymore.

The bar was still booming when I decided to take the stairs to the fifth floor; I figured that in the golden years, it would have been a penthouse suite for Mr. McLelland, but the fifth with a good view was fair dues for a former Hollywood Great who had been overtaken somewhat by the passing of time and cinematic violence, sex, and special effects.

I'm a grown man now, but my palms felt a little sweaty and my breathing was short and heavy when I tapped lightly on the door – and that was not just because of the stairs. Realizing it was a hesitant sort of introduction, I knocked a little louder, and I heard movement, unhurried, and then the door was opened in a deliberate fashion.

I was kind of shocked because upon first impression, Mr. McLelland was exactly as I recall him on celluloid and how my daddy had described him; in fact, he was taller in reality than I had imagined him to be – he seemed neither shrunken nor bowed with age, and he had a casual, confident bearing, while the hair was still copious and mostly dark. His eyes held humor amid the liquid hazel, and he smiled when he said –

"Hello, can I help you?"

Well, how should I have begun upon meeting someone my daddy had spoken of so frequently and glowingly? I told him the truth, as I knew it, and told him that I was sorry to bother him, but that he was someone whom I had admired (albeit vicariously), and that he knew my daddy well.

His face, lined, still aristocratically handsome, lit up pleasurably, and I could see that this was a kind man.

"Oh? Why, then, come in Mr....? Davies did you say?"

"Yes sir. My da... that is, my father's name is Thomas, but they all called him Tom."

He mulled this over as he invited me in, pouring me a bourbon with ice when I nodded at his glance and another for himself, and we sat opposite each other on two high-backed and prissy chairs. Finally, he crossed one leg over the other and said –

"I'll say the name is not striking any bells with me right now, Mr. Davies – but then, when you get to my age, that's hardly surprising." He smiled as he said this. "Where exactly did your father and I meet?"

Well, that could have set me off, but I held on tight to my eagerness and merely told him that my daddy was a cameraman, *the* cameraman, his favourite cameraman, the one he had shared so many evenings on film sets and locations with. At that he frowned slightly, though not in

an unpleasant way; it seemed to me as though he were mulling over what I had said. He put his fingers to his lips and stroked them before he began –

"I'm sorry, Mr. Davies, I just don't..." He paused and slowly looked over at me, then snapped his fingers as though he could have kicked himself for his forgetfulness and started again –

"Goodness! Why, of *course* I remember Tom – a plague on my memory, Mr. Davies! Forgive me, we worked together on the Warner Brothers lot, didn't we? Yes, and Fox. Well, well..." and he was off. He told me so many yarns of the illustrious and the famous, always throwing in my daddy's name – I felt that I was once again listening at my daddy's knee, except that it was he who was at the centre and the movie stars were merely bit part players.

47

He topped my drink up several times and bestrode the room while he talked, sometimes animated, occasionally reflective – the conversation turning sometimes upon a question I might have asked or an observation I'd made. All of a sudden, he stopped as a porcelain mantle clock struck the midnight hour, and he looked surprised, then rueful.

"Well, goodness I cannot believe the time!" He sank, fairly exhausted, into a chair and bade forgiveness while he laughed and said that at his age sleep was one of his necessities as well as one of his pleasures.

"Although", he nodded and spoke in a quiet voice, "it has indeed been a pleasure talking with you about your father."

I looked at him; he appeared frail and worn, and I suddenly felt guilty for having kept that kindly man from his rest. I sprang to my feet.

"I cannot thank you enough, Mr. McLelland." I shook his hand, and despite appearances, his grip was still firm. I was moving towards the door when he stopped me.

"Just one minute, please."

He went to a walnut bureau near the window – no doubt he used that oftentimes to write or read his scripts whilst staying at this hotel – opened it and pulled out a large photograph. He held it up, and it was an old studio shot of himself in one of his most famous poses; the fact that it was monochrome only added to the Hollywood allure and mystique of those days that would not return, when stars really were stars. His slightly aquiline features were distinct, his black hair made glossier by the stock-quality photographic paper, and his eyes, though not in colour, still held that hidden glimmer, a sprinkling of stardust.

"I wonder if your fath… your daddy… would like a memento of our meeting, a reminder of times past?"

I smiled. "He certainly would, Mr. McLelland."

He uncapped an exquisite-looking pen, and I thought that it was the sort of pen only actors of a certain age would own. Placing the photo on the bureau desk, he wrote without hesitation and in a wonderful hand: *"To my dear friend Tom, happy memories. Yours, JM."*

The next morning, I headed home to Nevada and left my crew to finish off. To be honest, I felt as though I'd had my fill of the mundane and the inglorious, and though I knew TV was where the money was,

I had an idea, or perhaps it was merely a wish, that film, and Hollywood in particular, were due a comeback; I certainly hoped so because that's where I planned to head.

I drove straight to the home where Daddy was staying; it was clean, the gardens were green and fecund with splashes of colour, and the staff were kindly and generous with their time with the patients – it was something I paid for, and that made my TV work worthwhile. The home was all that could be hoped for, though I was never too sure of how much Daddy was aware of things on a daily basis.

His room was a pretty one – light, airy, and with a comfortable chair overlooking the gardens, and when I knocked and entered, that's exactly where he was sitting; it was only when I got closer that I saw his eyes were closed. The curtains were partially drawn and were swaying to a light breeze while the sun played around the room, and I gently shook him awake. His eyes looked directly at me but not in any meaningful way; I can only describe that look as bemused or perplexed – he somehow understood that he *should* know me. That look frightened me, so I talked in a soft voice about things past until there came a point when a hint of recognition came happily into his eyes, and he reached out and clasped my hand with a smile; it was then that I told him about my meeting with Mr. McLelland.

Well, he lit up in a way that was good to see – Hollywood had that effect on him – and paid great attention, nodding his head as he listened. When I produced the photo signed so elegantly, he read the inscription and quietly said – "That Mr. McLelland, he could *act,* yes he could."

I thought back to the puzzled look in the actor's eyes and how he had looked at me, and I guess, perhaps, he had seen in that astute, quick-minded way of his that he was somehow looking at a small boy whose dreams were about to fall through the floor, whose belief in truth and in someone he cared so much about was about to collapse like the house of cards that Hollywood itself was.

"He is the best actor I ever saw," I said.

"He's a great star, son", he murmured as he laid his head back and closed his eyes; he held the photograph close to his chest and smiled.

"He's an even greater man," I murmured and watched my Daddy sleep.

49

THE HORSEMEN RIDING BY

"Are you sure you heard a trumpet?" Pestilence asked irritably of Famine.

The four horsemen sat overlooking the World. Despite its vast height, the mountain was not snow-capped, almost bare; there were no clouds below to obscure their view of what appeared to be a green and pleasant land stretching out before them. They all looked extremely disappointed at this idyllic scene.

"Well," Famine began nervously, "I'm pre-e-tty sure I heard one, but..."

Pestilence exploded. "Pretty sure?!" He turned to Death. "Did you hear that, Mr. D? Pretty sure he says! What the hell," he made the sign of a slit throat when he said this, "are we doing here then?!"

"Oh goodness..." Famine started to defend himself, but War cracked up at this and hooted with laughter.

"Goodness? What's goodness got to do with anything, you idiot?" he cackled as he slapped his mighty horse, which was as red as blood itself.

The lugubrious Mr. D, Death himself, shook his head and merely remained silent – his grey eyes searching the long reaches of the Earth. Waiting.

Pestilence turned back to Famine. "Get that book out, you dolt, and let's have a read of what's going on. I swear you've been starving your brain along with everything else."

Famine sighed and reached into his saddle bag. His horse, darker than a cosmic black hole from which no light could escape, stood patiently as he ferreted about. Secretly, he was proud of his mount – he thought even Mr. D's stallion, a sort of pasty pale in his view, could not compare, and he absentmindedly patted its neck as he pulled out a small book covered with black leather and gilded with gold. A red "R" flamed in its centre.

He thumbed through the Book of Revelation, wishing that Pestilence wasn't quite such a grumpikins, and came to Chapter 6.

"Okay, here we are... Oh goodness, I didn't hear a trumpet after all," he confessed. Both War and Pestilence tightened their lips and looked at each other. War, in addition, hefted his massive sword and looked as though he wanted to make good use of it.

"No, no, it's okay," Famine hurriedly continued with relief, "we are right where and when we should be. That trumpet doesn't sound until we have done our bit. This is interesting, though," he frowned.

"Yeah? I can't wait. Please, pray tell," said Pestilence with sarcasm.

"It says we *are given power over a fourth of the world to kill by sword, famine, and plague and by the wild beasts of the Earth'.* A fourth? That's a quarter, isn't it? What's happened to the other half?"

Pestilence muttered and shook his head, covering his face with his hands whilst War roared, "Give me that damned book, you idiot!"

Famine hastily threw him the book, and War thumbed through it to the right page and scanned it swiftly. He fell silent.

Reluctantly, he turned to Pestilence. "The fool is right," then he continued, "but if anyone thinks that I'm going to be satisfied with only a fourth..." he paused, ominously. They all looked at each other and nodded, slowly.

Suddenly, Mr. D, who had been silent all of this time, raised his arm deliberately and pointed with a long white finger, gnarled since time began.

"There," he said softly.

Four pairs of eyes looked towards the distant North West – it was only a small white cloud that spiralled from the ground, but it formed a mushroom-like shape, and a few moments later, a sonic boom rolled across the green plain and rose up to meet them. They waited for the scorching wind to follow.

"And there," Death pointed his finger again, this time to the East. Their eyes swung rapidly to and fro as they endeavoured to keep pace with a tennis match that was being played with atomic balls and with deadly abandon and which could have no winner.

"It's time," Death decided, and they each pulled their cowls, white, black, red, and ashen, away from their faces – the better for humanity to see their fate.

"Oh yeah," said Pestilence.

"Oh goodness," mumbled Famine.

"Yippee ki yay, mother fu...", began War when Death stopped him sharply.

51

"No need for bad language!" he said. They all looked at him, and he suddenly grinned while they cracked up laughing.

The Four Horsemen of the Apocalypse swept down through the valleys of the Earth, all four fourths of it, and there was very little left by the time the trumpet finally sounded.

JUST A SHORT WALK

I can still see Mary's cottage from my own, though my eyes are not what they used to be. I must tread the clifftop path ever further before it draws fully into focus, although I can visualise it with ease – it's whitewashed walls covered with creeping ivy, the leaded windows, opaque, with curtains of cream hung inside, the small garden where we often sat and laughed facing the deserted lighthouse on the Point that once preserved lives threatened by the rocks and the leaping, spraying, thundering waves in the bay below.

Lily breathes heavily as she pads alongside me; we grow old together and blow hard together as we tread the familiar path. This mile, from the beachfront to the clifftop – from my home to Mary's, next to the greensward with the booming sea below us on our right – wearies my body now but never my soul.

Although there is less spring in her Spaniel steps, she still has the old swing of her tail and her eyes are still bright and loving. She is an intelligent dog; perhaps she, too, recalls how it all began.

Let me sit here at the mid-point, at the bench where Mary and I watched the sun drop below the pink-hued sea. Let me close my eyes and live it all over again.

The cottage had been deserted for many years, which always surprised me given its barren beauty and its aspect. For the right person with the right heart, at one with the hidden but living soul of the wind and the sea, no more could be asked of a home.

Myself? Well, firstly, I could not afford it and, to be frank, I recognised myself for what I was – rather leaden, intelligent enough and content, after a lifetime in the city, with my books, my dog, a little socialising, but not too much. I came to recognise the metaphor construed in these two cottages – me at the foot of the cliffs, sunken, and Mary, elevated and free. Each footstep towards the summit raised me higher both physically and spiritually.

We first met at the mid-point of the cliff where we were to meet so many times. Her Springer Spaniel, Jake, was perilously close to the edge, and I held him firmly while Mary nonchalantly smiled and thanked me. The two dogs were smitten instantly; if there is a doggy "love at first sight", it happened that day.

We met often after that. At first, it was unintentional on my part, but I realised after a while that my hands shook when I whistled to Lily for her walk. On Mary's part, I entertained no illusion that there was any such anticipation. She was always cool, always polite, and yet as time moved forward, she opened up and shared her thoughts – WE shared our thoughts.

Neither of us was young, but there the similarity ended; she was a free spirit, she had travelled and still did. Her beauty came from her openness, living for the moment, being at one with whatever pleased her soul. One might say she was Bohemian, although she liked some luxuries but never to excess. She cared not for superficialities. We walked, we sat in her garden, we drank wine, we laughed. She showed me her paintings, and more than once, she drew or painted the lighthouse for which she had a joyous fascination, often looking at it for long periods as we sat on this same bench, watching the sea break at its jagged base.

The first time she said she was going away, my heart lurched. She laughed and told me not to look so crestfallen, that she would be back.

She returned after 5 months. I felt, without knowing, that she was back, and Lily and I strode anxiously to the clifftop. There, with a laugh and a wave, she and Jake met us as if it had been only the day before that we had parted.

With each passing year, the time she spent away lessened. Our bones aged in tandem; the walks and the dogs became slower. Time could never completely take away the restless spirit in her eyes, but I could see something as near to contentment in them as I ever would.

We never spoke of love; I'm not sure she would have understood it as I would. Besides, I am sometimes a selfish, impatient man, I am at least aware enough to know that; what right had I to contain that impetuous life?

The day Mary told me she was going away and would not be coming back, it was a bright May day – the anticipation of summer in the air. Lily had managed to run to her as she saw Jake and her treading the path, both greyer and slower like ourselves. I wish that I had run to her that day too. I did not understand why she was leaving... leaving me.

54

I am tying Lily up firmly to the bench – I can't have her slipping the leash – and she has grown quiet. She always was intelligent, she understands me. I give her one final stroke, and tell her I love her.

The plaque on the bench reads – "Mary Mortimer, a free spirit come home to rest. 1940–2016".

I turn my back and walk the few steps towards the cliff edge. I can see the lighthouse across the bay, and I set my face resolutely towards it – the waves below drum a beating heart… two beating hearts. I am an impatient man, Mary, I'm sorry I can't wait… It's just a short walk, Mary…

DUEL IN THE BOIS DE VINCENNES

Francois-Etienne, Comte de Montfore, watched as his betrothed flirted outrageously with a gaggle of young *noblesse*; it particularly irked him that the Marquis de Dubois was among them. He turned to his two companions and attempted to continue his conversation. "As I was saying, I..."

A laugh, gay but hardly bell-like, rose to the chandeliers and all three *aristos* flinched. Pierre, the young Vicomte de Marsat, was privately glad that his friend's fiancée was standing at the far end of the room. Attractive as Mademoiselle Charlotte, daughter of the Duc de Bruiset was, he believed that even the advantages of beauty and breeding could not outweigh her two faults; namely, her capricious nature and total lack of intellect.

The Comte tried once more. "As I was saying..." The laugh rang out again, and this time the Comte reddened.

"Mon Dieu! What can the Marquis and his unruly *copains* possibly be saying that prompts such a laugh! It is unseemly, it is disgraceful, it is..."

"Utterly normal for the young Mademoiselle," laughed Henri, the third of the trio. The least ennobled, merely a Baron, he was at least the most sensible. He was aware of how hot blooded the Comte was and always did his best to keep him in check; he had saved his honour, and probably his life, on several occasions.

All three of them turned to look at the Marquis. Undoubtedly, he was the centre of attention, and the men – a veritable pride of peacocks in their bright red or blue swallow -tailed coats, made fashionable by their monarch Louis XVI – emulated his easy, confident manner; not least in order to attract the bevy of the Mademoiselles, the Duc's daughter key amongst them, who surrounded him. Of course, all knew that marriage ambitions were driven by the need to preserve and attain influence and riches, not to mention status; but if one could just find a single potential partner that did not look like the hind end of a *cochon*, how grateful they would be!

Irritated as the Comte was at the Mademoiselle's behaviour – and embarrassed too it must be said – all would have been well, had the Marquis not, at that precise moment, leaned over and whispered something that clearly made her face flush and those wonderful blue eyes shine like dew on a lily. The Comte raged, "He exceeds the bounds of propriety *mes amis*, I will speak with him!"

His friends looked at each other, and Henri addressed the Comte languidly.

"Now, now Francois, do not be hasty. Honour is one thing, but a little frivolous conversation need not be a motivation for friction between the scions of two respectable families. And besides," he continued swiftly when he saw how serious Francois was, "you must be aware that the Marquis de Dubois is reputed to be the finest swordsman from Normandy to Lorraine."

Henri, no mean swordsman himself, was aware that the Comte – even after having taken the tutorage obliged by all nobles in the art of fencing – was still no more than adequate, and as a pistol shot, mediocre at best.

"And in addition…" began Pierre, but it was too late. The Comte was already striding towards the group where the Marquis – almost a full head taller than the others – stood holding court in his easy going way. As the Comte approached, the babble of chatter increased and another burst of laughter broke out. All of this infuriated Francois and drove him to distraction, but propriety forbade him from giving full rein to his feelings.

As he approached the group, the Marquis turned and when he saw Francois, bowed and bade him welcome. "Ah, Monsieur le Comte, come and join us!"

He swept a hospitable arm towards the group. His white shirt cuffs were turned up closely against the red sleeves of his coat; he eschewed any of the flamboyant embroidery of the previous decade, and his coat and waistcoat had merely narrow braids and simple silver garlands, while his small sword, his *epee de cour*, swung loosely at his waist. He was the height of fashion.

Francois, to be fair, was as elegantly attired himself; dressed in blue, with the latest style *collet* at his neck, and in his own way as handsome as the Marquis; both of them were bewigged and delicately powdered. To those who did not know them, however, first impressions would always be that the Comte had a somewhat sour face, particularly when irked, whilst the Marquis always had an air of *bonhomie*.

The Comte bowed shortly and set his attentions to the Mademoiselle.

"Mademoiselle Charlotte, I believe it is time to leave. I promised your father that I would escort you home at a reasonable hour."

Charlotte looked petulant; from across the room, Pierre mentally added 'difficult' to her list of faults. "Oh, but Monsieur...Francois... I am having such a good time – let us stay a while longer!"

"But Mademoiselle", Francois tried to assert himself, but the Marquis laughed indulgently.

"There, Monsieur le Comte, it appears the lady is enjoying herself. You may have to tell the Duc that his daughter is of a strong will. However, I'm sure he is aware of that!"

Francois, red faced, spoke directly to the Marquis, "Kindly allow me, Monsieur, to speak with my fiancée without interruption. Now, Mademoiselle..."

"I think you have had your answer already Monsieur le Comte," said the Marquis. Rather presumptuously, although in good humour, he added, "I think that your residency with the Mademoiselle is going to be a fiery one!"

He turned his back on the Comte and muttered a few words to his companions, at which they all burst into laughter.

It was too much for Francois; and before he realised what he was saying, and the consequences of his words, said in a cold voice, "You insult me Monsieur – I demand satisfaction!"

The little crowd went quiet. The Marquis turned around slowly, with a look of astonishment on his face. "You...demand satisfaction Monsieur!"

Now reluctant, but keeping a bold front, Francois reiterated his point, "I do indeed, Monsieur le Marquis."

The Marquis, generally a well-intentioned man, could hardly

refuse; although a veteran of several duels and having nothing to prove, to decline - particularly before a throng of his admirers - would be tantamount to an act of cowardice. And a coward he most certainly was not.

"Well, well, Monsieur le Comte, if you so insist, I will await your seconds," he bowed and returned to his conversation.

Now feeling somewhat at a loss, Francois was joined quickly by Pierre and Henri, and realising the gravity of the situation, Charlotte came to his side. Although she was taken aback by the turn of events, both of the Comte's friends noticed how her eyes shone. To have two such nobles duelling over her, as she saw it, was a matter of delight – the serious consequences simply did not occur to her – and although unusually quiet in her carriage as she was escorted home, she tightly held her fiancé's arm and whispered to him how brave he was; then she swiftly fell asleep, dreaming of flashing swords. It has to be said that Francois did not sleep so soundly.

*

It was the early morning of the duel. Two days prior, the Comte's major second, Henri, had written to the Marquis' equivalent outlining the extent of the grievance. He had requested an apology from the Marquis for the slight afforded the Comte – if forthcoming, the duel would be called off. No one seriously expected such an apology – the Marquis had already accepted the challenge in public – and it had remained only to agree to the particulars.

As was customary, the challenged party had the choice of weapons for combat and the Marquis opted for rapiers. The field of honour was a hidden clearing in the Bois de Vincennes, two kilometres thence, just east of Paris. The time was set at dawn, as was customary, mainly to avoid the authorities; duelling was strictly forbidden under law and had been since the reign of Louis XIII. However, in many instances, a blind eye was turned, unless carried out blatantly.

For Francois, the only silver lining around this dark cloud of his own creation, was that Henri had specified that the duel would be fought only until first blood was drawn. Although perilous enough, it meant that the prospect of death was ameliorated; even though the many who had fought under this code might have argued with this – had they been alive to do so.

59

Having ridden to the Bois de Vincennes with the sun yet to rise, Pierre and Henri carried lanterns that lit the path to the isolated clearing. Francois was fully aware that this had been the scene of several infamous duels; he wondered how much of his own blood might be spilled to mingle with that of other unfortunates. When they arrived, he saw that the Marquis and his seconds were already there, along with a surgeon and two witnesses.

With little ado – and following the rejection of last-minute appeals by the seconds on both sides – the protagonists, formally dressed but without their coats, each chose one of the two proffered swords, bowed, and began the duel.

It was a *fiasco*.

It was evident that Francois was no swordsman, and that the Marquis was as good as his reputation said; had honour not been involved, such a match would never have taken place. Even so, Francois thrust and cut with vigour, each stroke becoming more desperate – his shirt dripping with sweat even in the early morning chill - whilst the Marquis calmly parried and rarely attacked – a sardonic eyebrow raised – until he became bored and using an elegantly carried out *riposte*, made a deliberate thrust to the Comte's sword arm causing a dash of red to flower on his white shirt. Francois yelled and dropped his sword.

"Blood!" cried Henri and quickly came between them. The Marquis lowered his sword and stepped forward.

"Is your honour satisfied Monsieur?" he asked. Although fuming, Francois – his pride hurting much more than his wound – was in no position to gainsay it and nodded.

No more words were spoken. As the seconds and witnesses gathered the equipment, coats and horses and the surgeon attended to Francois' forearm, Henri glanced over towards his friend - he did not like what he saw. There was a look in the Comte's usually petulant and weak eyes that he had never seen before – it was one of fury and stubbornness and had a steely quality that did not bode well for the future – whose future he was not sure of yet. Francois glared at the Marquis' back as he rode away on a chestnut mare. The horse's flanks rippled and shone in the bright light of the sun, its rays finally reaching the scene of what was a *debacle*; but which could have been something more deadly had the Marquis so wished.

When Pierre and Henri called upon Francois the next day, they were told that he had gone away; he did not return for eight months.

*

It was a night when the cold wind swept with a terrible vitality through the streets and alleyways of Paris; the rich had sense enough to remain indoors, and the poor found protection from its bitterness wherever they could. Rain beat down against turret and window alike, and it was a melancholy game of *piquet* that Pierre and Henri played in the latter's *salon* at his town house in the district of Marais. Neither party mentioned Francois, but he was never far from their thoughts; he had not been seen since the day of the duel, though rumour had it that he was in England – his estate and town house had been kept up mostly through the good offices and oversight of his two friends.

Restless, Henri finally threw down his *jeu de cartes* and walked to the window, lost in thought. At that moment, a servant knocked and entered, announcing that a visitor was awaiting them.

"At this hour?" Both companions raised their eyebrows and Henri signalled the servant to present the visitor, but before he could do so, a shrouded, saturated figure swept in; and after shaking the rain from himself threw back his cowl.

Pierre and Henri leapt to their feet. "Francois!" they exclaimed together.

The Comte stood before them. He was unshaven and had no wig; his hair was tangled and wet and gave him the appearance of a vagabond of the street. However, he laughed the same laugh that they knew so well, but which he too infrequently used. Only Henri noticed that he had the same wild light in his eyes that he had seen after the duel.

Having sat him down and provided him with a warming brandy the two friends extracted from him the details they desired – although when he had finished, both of them silently decided that the answers were not the ones they would have liked to have heard.

Francois had sailed to England the day after the duel. He had sought out Domenico Angelo, the great Italian fencing master and had enrolled in his renowned School of Arms in Eton; more, he had entreated Angelo to provide him with months of painstaking personal

61

tuition – at great cost it had to be said.

"Mon Dieu! What a genius the man is. *Mes amis*, I will tell you this, when I meet the Marquis in combat again, the result will be somewhat different than before!"

"When you…when you…meet the Marquis?" stuttered Henri. He looked aghast, and Pierre paled.

"But of course! Why else would I spend months on that island of the uncouth, away from my friends, my estates and Mademoiselle Charlotte? I do not take humiliation lightly", and the Comte's face darkened.

At the mention of Charlotte, Pierre and Henri looked at each other in a furtive manner and Pierre hesitantly began, "Francois, I need to tell you…"

"Oh, *sacre bleu* Pierre do not worry!" interrupted Francois impatiently. "Henri, take up your small sword."

Henri looked extremely doubtful at this request, not because he was unsure of his own prowess, but because of the look in Francois' eyes, which seemed to be taking on an expression akin to madness by the minute.

"Francois…"

"Come, come Henri!" the Comte began to redden.

Henri shrugged his shoulders and reached for his sword, which was leaning by the window. He peered out at streets glistening with rain that continued to fall heavily and the wind whistled at the pane; he wondered where this lunacy was going to end.

He turned however, smiling.

"*En guarde* Francois", he said.

Henri was shocked. The skill with which Francois twisted and turned his blade had Henri at the full stretch of his own capabilities; within a few strokes Henri was backed up against the wall – a simple *tierce,* followed by a lightening, circular motion of Francois' sword and Henri was disarmed with the tip at his throat; for a second he believed that he was a dead man, but Francois lowered his sword and merely laughed delightedly.

"There Henri! *Epee*, small sword, rapier, sabre – it matters not what the Marquis chooses, I am his superior. I need only a reason to challenge him and Charlotte will see who is the master…yes…who is the...who is..." he shook his head, as if not sure where he was.

Pierre began to speak slowly, whilst Henri, shaken, poured himself a brandy.

"Francois...Mademoiselle Charlotte...she...she is no longer your fiancée. You cannot blame her *mon ami* – you went away without a word; no one knew where you were..." he tailed off; then said slowly, "She is now engaged to the Marquis de Dubois!"

Francois-Etienne, the Comte de Montfore, stood frozen. His face and neck flushed purple and Henri noticed two pulses beating, one at his temple and the other beneath his left ear. There was stillness and silence for a full minute; it was a *tableau* of three nobles and two of them at least were frightened about what might happen next.

But instead, the Comte merely said, "Perfect."

*

It was evening. Two days had passed since Francois' return and once again the three men sat in Henri's salon; the Comte in an agitated state and the others merely resigned. Neither of them had been present when Francois, the evening after his arrival – shaved, bathed and clothed resplendently – had called upon the Marquis as he sat down to dinner with his friends at his residence in the *Place des Vosges* – Mademoiselle Charlotte among them.

Such an intrusion was an insult in itself and the Marquis would have been quite within his rights to have had the Comte removed. However, in his usual relaxed and tolerant fashion, he had called for an additional chair. The Comte, pointedly looking at the terrified Charlotte and then at the Marquis, had no desire to be placated – he had only one aim – to issue a challenge to duel; and unjustifiable as it was, used the Mademoiselle's change of favour as an excuse. He babbled some words about duplicity, taking advantage of his absence, and removing his glove, threw it down in front of the Marquis.

To his credit, the Marquis calmly removed the glove from his soup and suggested that he would arrange for it to be cleaned; but all present knew that such an affront could not be ignored. He had then said simply, in a soft voice, "We have been here before, Monsieur. But I await your seconds," and, with composure, he continued with his meal. Those around him saw, however, that there was a deadly coldness about him, reflected in the rigidity of his jaw and in his eyes.

Now, a knock at the salon door had Francois leaping to his feet. At his insistence, Henri had issued the formal challenge; Francois had demanded that he ensure it was a duel fought to the death. Henri had seen little point in arguing – Francois seemed to have tipped over into insanity.

The servant brought over a letter with the terms and handed it to Henri, who waited for the servant to retreat and then opened it. He went very quiet.

"What is it Henri?" the Comte almost shouted. "He has agreed, has he not? The Bois de Vincennes? As before…it must be as it was before!"

"Yes," replied Henri.

"And? The weapons Henri, the weapons. Is it to be rapiers? I so want it to be rapiers!"

Pierre looked at Henri's face and sat suddenly; he shivered though there was a fire burning in the hearth.

"It is…pistols, Francois," said Henri.

The Comte continued as if he had not heard. "I don't mind if it is an *epee* or sabre. Henri, I am his master. Even small swords will do, though they are not worthy of such a duel."

"Pistols." Henri said firmly and with finality.

"But he cannot…I…I…have worked so hard…he…I…"

The Comte sat down; and though there was silence, they all thought they heard Death sing his eternal *chanson*.

Henri stood by his friend and placed a hand on his shoulder. *"La vie, ca pue,"* he said.

"I tried to tell you Francois, I really did, when you challenged him before," said Pierre. "The Marquis is the finest swordsman from Normandy to Lorraine…*but he is the best pistol shot in France!"*

*

Epilogue

The Comte was killed with a single shot between the eyes, which enhanced the Marquis' reputation further as a master of the duel.

The Marquis was arrested and imprisoned for murder, but released after three months following appeals and evidence of provocation.

Mademoiselle Charlotte married someone else entirely; a young noble from outside Paris, who was a pacifist.

TIME AHEAD

As he lay in bed, the clock ticked once, and its hands moved.

He thought, *"Time is movement; without movement, Time would stand still. Even thought is movement".*

He raised his head slightly and saw that the sun had finally struggled through the mid-morning cloud. There were dark hints that it would rain later in the day; this was enough to make him feel that he probably wouldn't go out today – no, not even to the shops.

He moved his gaze and saw that the hands of the ebony, Kaufmann crafted clock, gifted to him upon his reluctant retirement, stood at 5 minutes to 10. In his mind's eye, he saw himself creep reluctantly from beneath his warm bedclothes, shuffle to the bathroom, shave (*or should he really bother?*), and shower in hot water that would splash steamily against the fashionable Italian porcelain tiles, casually paid for with the fruits of his until recently high-powered and highly paid labour.

He reminisced about how he would ready himself for work at a dash; swiftly throwing on one of his five tailored suits, one purchased for each working day. Always immaculate, despite the rush, he would have consumed the percolated coffee made and left ready by his wife (he would never drink instant even when he was hurried) and then wolf down his croissant as he ran out of the door. But he would have to do that no more. This morning, he would once again linger alone over his breakfast, boil a kettle, and, with a vacant expression on his face, he would watch the steam condense and turn into droplets that would collect and slide sluggishly down the wall to accrue on the marble work surface.

He idly wondered whether he should telephone Stuart at his former office and arrange to meet for lunch one day, although he recalled the undertones of previous calls and envisaged Stuart glancing up and down at his PC, tapping at the keys feverishly with one hand whilst holding the phone with the other, and absentmindedly conversing, but with little interest, making jokes about how he had been held up by yet another pensioner in the supermarket who had searched for his pennies. No, he could not face another pained conversation like that.

He thought of the day ahead. He considered the early night drawing in at the end of another slow, wasted day. He also considered the emptiness he would feel until his wife finished work and returned home from London; and he then concluded that Time was, in fact, decay or at the least the cause of it.

He turned over, closed his eyes, and slept. Time stood still again.

THE SPOON

I'll tell you what happened to me as a kid once – it was just that one time.

It was a Sunday evening, and Uri Geller was on television, bending spoons – through the power of his mind, as he claimed. It irritated a lot of people (other magicians and conjurors, mainly), and still does, that he always insisted it was authentic. He maintained he didn't really know how he did it – it just happened.

He was about to perform the feat again, and I kept a shrewd, close eye on his hands. I knew what to look for: the sleight of hand, the misdirection. It seemed that the cameraman, like me, was determined not to miss a thing; the lens was focused and inquisitive, projecting a picture that was close up and large on the screen.

I've always been fascinated by magic, conjuring, or whatever else you like to call it. For a kid, I wasn't bad at it – I'd already exhausted the children's library and moved on to reading the more serious stuff about magic. The books piled on my bureau – Modern Coin Magic, Daryl's Card Revelations, Tarbell's Complete Course in Magic – were evidence of my fascination, but none of them satisfactorily taught me how to bend cutlery and make it melt at my fingertips, to seemingly make it fall apart in my hands. The methods I had read about just did not seem to fit the bill – when Uri Geller performed, it just seemed so...*real*.

I focused my attention on the television and watched as Uri gently stroked the stem of what looked, at least to me, like a pretty sturdy tablespoon made of steel. Admittedly, it was at the point where the stem met the shiny bowl; a point that was certain to be the weakest on the spoon, but his fingers appeared to exert little pressure. He seemed, in fact, to do little more than caress the metal, before the bowl began to gradually curve upwards. He pulled it down with delicate fingers, then up, and then down again. Each time, the spoon looked more fragile, like heated plastic. All of a sudden the bowl came off in his fingers – there was nothing severe about the process, it just seemed to effortlessly ease away from the stem.

I asked myself (and hated the fact that I did so) the involuntary question that always crops up when a magician does something seemingly impossible – how the hell did he do that?

As luck would have it, Mum entered the room behind me, carrying a case of silver-plated cutlery. She told me to polish it in readiness for our dinner guests that evening. Generally speaking, the only expectation my mum had from spoons, forks, or knives was for them to be clean and ready to eat with. I rose, switched off the TV, and cast a slightly peeved eye at my collection of books, before sitting down at the dining room table.

The cutlery set was actually quite stylish, even to my youthful eye. Each silver clad handle was embellished with an arcane pattern. The spoon that I picked up seemed substantial and heavy, and I wondered what Uri Geller would have made of it. I held the spoon in my left hand, and, with a fragment of cleaning cloth in my right, I exhaled on the stem and bowl and absentmindedly began to massage it to a highly polished sheen.

I kind of got into a rhythm, so, by the time I reached the seventh spoon, I wasn't really looking at it or thinking about much in general. It therefore came as a bit of a shock to me when I put it down next to its table-mates and noticed that it looked sort of…different. It seemed to be standing proudly on the table with a slight arch to it. I examined it more closely, and the more I looked, I felt that the bowl at the end of the spoon was winking at me in a sardonic manner – a shining, oval eye.

I picked it up and held it to the light and then compared it closely to another spoon – there was, no doubt, a distinct curve.

I held it gently, then more firmly, as I rolled my fingertips together along top and bottom, smoothly, soothingly, then wonderingly. It began to feel warm to the touch, and then almost hot. At first it felt malleable and clay-like, then it felt as you might imagine Mercury to feel – globular, then frustratingly ungraspable. It got to the point where it couldn't hold itself together. This ordinary piece of metal was defying the rules of the universe as I had always perceived them. The atoms parted, and the bowl clunked to the table.

I sat there in silence for a while, the stem of the spoon held limbless in my right hand, while I stared at the bowl, and it stared back at me.

68

Then Mum came into the room, whistling.

Now, when my mum says *"jump"*, you jump, and when she shouts at you, you know you've been shouted at. Fundamental shifts in the laws of physics are pretty impossible to explain even at the best of times, but before a harangue like that, my lips could only open and close like a fish, while Mum gave me the full benefit of her tongue. My mind was in a state of numbness, but the occasional word or phrase hit me - *broken heirloom, Gran, Father, kill you* – then, finally – *"Up to bed and NO DINNER!"*

I was feeling pretty sorry for myself by the time I dragged myself upstairs and flung down on the bed. I was hungry, magic or no magic, distortions in laws of physics or not. I lay there, full of both wonder and annoyance.

There was a teaspoon in a cup on a small table next to my bed, and when I noticed it, I sat up sharply and gazed at it indecisively for a long while. Finally, curiosity got the better of me, and I picked it up.

Well, could I get that spoon to bend? The heck I could! The Universe, or someone in it, on top of it, or around it, had allowed me to break its concrete rules – just the once. I came to the conclusion this was a good thing, as I hate missing dinner. I also can't keep paying for broken spoons out of my pocket money – Uri Geller earns a lot more than I do.

A VIEW TO AN END

It seemed likely to him that this was going to be a difficult and troubling evening.

The waiter, solicitous and, at the same time, indifferent, led him to the corner table where she sat, nodded shortly, and left him facing her. Standing alone in that crowded room, he watched her.

She was texting, her eyes down, with slow and deliberate fingers. Her lips were narrowed and pinched at the ends, but not enough to disguise the fullness that had always drawn him to her. His expression softened and his lips relaxed into a smile. Sensing his presence, she raised her head and caught this. He wished she hadn't.

She immediately smiled nervously in return as he pulled up a chair and sat down to bring himself to her level. His phone pinged and announced the delivery of her text in his pocket, and he ignored it.

"I was about to leave, Phil," she said, "but I'm glad you came."

Ruthlessness was not in his nature; he said nothing more until he had ordered two small Merlots from the sommelier waiting politely at their side. His chest tightened at the thought of what he had to impart, but they had always been straight – at least with each other.

Small talk is difficult when you have important things to say, but he did his best to keep it flowing and casual and light. His hand was steady whenever he raised his glass, yet his knees were tense and rigid beneath the table. He kept his eyes averted from hers for as long he could, taking his time to peruse the red leather and gold leafed menu and finally ordering for them both her favourite *a la carte* dish of fillet of turbot braised in red wine. He could not help but feel that was an attempt on his part to assuage his guilt for what he was about to do. He wondered, *was this a final meal for a condemned woman, or was he setting her free?* It was a silly, melodramatic reflection, and he really could not lie to himself – it was only his own freedom that concerned him.

As they ate, he noted that she moved pieces of the fish to the edge of the blue, flower-adorned plate and took frequent, restless sips from her glass. Although she conversed animatedly at first about all and nothing (neither interested him), there came a moment when the pure, clear

70

voice that had whispered to him of love and of her dreams as they lay in secret places – faltered, and both of them fell silent.

Their eyes met and softened as they gazed at each other, and he knew that it was time to say what he had come to say.

"I..."

She stood, put her still folded napkin next to his, leaned down, and placed those full lips briefly on his, whilst a long, white hand lightly rested on his shoulder. She then brushed past him towards the door, leaving him sitting, dazed and still, with his back toward the exit. He felt a cold draught behind him and an emptiness inside him, and he knew she was gone.

It took a little while for him to move, finally prompted by the waiter who showed concern at the little eaten food and fussed around and about until he assured him that the food was marvellous, the wine excellent – it was just that the lady had not been hungry.

He walked out unsteadily into the already dark evening. The streets were lit with pools of light beneath each stolid-looking lamp post, and the drizzle, even more pronounced in the gusty winds, was clearly visible until it merged into the darkness of the night.

He took his phone from his pocket and opened the text she had sent him before she was aware that he had arrived. And he knew that it said "Goodbye" - though he could not see it through eyes that he told himself were just blurred with the rain.

KING OF THE POOL

Before I was a writer, I was a kingmaker. Not many people can say that, can they? I don't mean it in a political sense, and I certainly didn't influence the course of the royal succession. No, it was in a minor way; but happening as it did during one long, hot summer in the course of my childhood, I was given an insight into the human nature and how a single incident can change a person and possibly the direction of their life.

My friends and I, along with the rest of the U.K., sweltered during the summer of 1983. It was not quite as fiery as 1976 but even so, the vast sun that seemed to inch across those cloudless, cobalt skies compelled us to take joyous refuge on a daily basis at the local lido. My friends and I, along with dozens of other school kids, were by turn listless or ebullient. We either baked or, after having leapt into the shockingly chill water of the pool, shivered. Each day, time seemed to idle while we played and splashed and dived and lay. Every glorious day we woke to vivid light, and when finally, we went home to sleep, it was with the sky barely dimmed.

A man walked into the lido on one of those days. He wore tiny black trunks and the sun seemed to project its rays directly onto his glowing, contoured torso as if he had his own personal sun bed. Our tans and bodies seemed insipid in comparison and we looked at each other appraisingly; all of us coming off a poor second. He had stomach muscles (I didn't know then that they were called "abs"), which were ridged and solid and every other muscle in his body seemed equally defined and in perfect proportion.

"King of the Pool," I muttered to one of my mates; the name spread and stuck.

Of course, he was much older than us, ancient in fact—all of 22 or so—but that didn't stop the teenage girls stealing looks while the boys ruined their tans going green with envy. As each day went by, however, he condescended to talk to us all, in between brushing his thick, sun-bleached hair in the poolside mirror, and he became one of us, albeit a "first among equals". Each day upon his arrival a buzz

72

would go around — "the King of the Pool is here" — and he would wave almost regally before placing his towel down carefully and laying amongst us.

I never really took to him myself, and that is not just a reflection in hindsight nor a result of jealousy at the time; I didn't like his arrogant, patronising manner, but more than that, I didn't like the way he treated Arnold.

Arnold served behind the kiosk at the lido; if you wanted a drink or a sandwich he was your man. He was tall, almost as tall as the King of the Pool himself, but that's where the similarity ended. He was lean, although scrawny might be a better description, wore spectacles and parted his limp hair on the girl's side, as it was then. It was ironic that his name was Arnold, as Schwarzenegger was just making a name for himself, and you couldn't imagine anyone less like him. However, he was inoffensive and just about tolerated by the kids, although some took the rise out of him. I always found him to be polite, and he invariably said hello to me; I occasionally wondered what it would be like to be in a dead-end job like that.

The strange thing is, the King of the Pool seemed to take a perverse shine to him, and Arnold, in turn, no doubt flattered by this attention, hung around with him during his breaks from serving. There was nothing sexual about this bond, and there was nothing equal about it either—the more I observed it, the less I liked it. Arnold always walked two steps behind the King of the Pool, who treated him much as you might treat a well-favoured pet, and more than once I heard a casual, foul-mouthed curse aimed at him. It was a demeaning role to play, although it was none of my business; and life as a kid had far more things to hold my attention. I, then, found out that life is also very unpredictable.

About a mile from the lido there ran a small canal with a path beside it. "Canal" was a turgid name for what was really just a sullied, urban beck, flowing, in the loosest sense of the word, for about two hundred metres. We never knew, or bothered to find out, where it originated from or where it finally ended; we only knew that the path alongside was a convenient way of getting home to our municipal estates where supper may or may not be available depending on the whims of our parents.

Four weeks into the holidays I found out how easy it was to drown. The canal path was irregularly strewn with the detritus of urban life—bottles, carrier bags, old house bricks—but cycling home from the lido as often as I did, I couldn't really blame this for falling in. I guess it was curiosity that caused it when I saw the King of the Pool and Arnold walking slightly ahead and I took my eye off the ground; I was in the water before I knew it, with the bike on top of me and my right foot trapped inside the chain.

I'm a strong swimmer—always have been—but there is a world of difference between swimming in a clean, albeit chlorinated, controlled environment with all your limbs free, and a murky, foul course of water, encumbered with clothes and a heavy steel bike. I could feel myself going under for the first time and just had time to shout for help.

I kept my eyes and mouth closed because I felt that if I swallowed any of that filthy water it was as likely to kill me as drowning. I struggled hard to get my head above the water, and when I did, I saw and heard something I will never forget.

The King of the Pool and Arnold were just above me at the side of the canal—they seemed to be arguing—and although in desperate straits, I wondered almost calmly why they weren't doing anything. Then, I heard the King of the Pool's voice distinctly: *"I can't swim!"*

I saw the shock on Arnold's face, and then, him wrenching off his shirt before I went under again.

*

I was at the lido early the next day. The evening before, my parents had been incredibly grateful to Arnold for saving my life, and, seemingly at least, unsympathetic towards me for falling in; there was also the little matter of the bike laying in the canal that they weren't too happy about. I'm guessing, though, that they were more pleased to see me than they let on.

Naturally, it was a tale that needed to be told. By 10 o'clock, as the sun and endless blue sky were once again promising to give us the sort of day we now took for granted, most of my friends knew and, as happens with these things, the word had swept around the already busy lido. I didn't think we would see the King of the Pool again.

I lay down, and a friend joined me and asked me about the rumour. I sat up to tell him that it was no rumour, and as I did so, I heard the buzz begin:

"The King of the Pool is here...the King of the Pool is here...the King of the Pool is here..." It started softly and got louder and louder until I felt the goosebumps rising on my arms.

My friend looked up, puzzled. "What are they going on about?" he said, "I can only see skinny old Arnold."

I looked up and waved to Arnold, who waved back. He was opening up the kiosk – but I had a feeling he was destined for better things.

I turned to my friend and said: "The King is dead mate; long live the King!"

HIGHER THAN GODS

One day, I stood upon a mountain. Steep in places, it was high enough such that, on a clear, hot autumn day in 1945, I could view three counties with ease from its summit.

It was a favourite place of mine, a place to contemplate and dream, although I never did know where one county ended and the others began – with their blended, bucolic fields of green and yellow and brown. Today, this was of no consequence. My eyes were set on the narrow, long path that looked buttery in the distance and flinty and white up close, whereupon a lone figure was striding purposefully towards me from the village and from beyond that, the farmhouse, far below. I sat waiting on an outcrop, which was sharp and grey and peppered with a mineral that sparkled in the sunlight.

Even a short distance on the hills can seemingly take a lifetime to traverse, and so, the figure grew larger only by degrees. I was patient, as I knew who it was. I smiled with a grimness. Those few comrades who observed that smile when I climbed into the cockpit called it *ill-disposed*. I think, however, that my actual feeling was a kind of bitter sadness. While I waited, I turned my slouch peak hat in my hands and then used it to brush the wind-swept summit dust from the shoulders and trousers of my uniform. It was blue-grey and heavy, and the heat beat down upon me, although I was cold inside – as only those who have been betrayed in love can feel.

Who could remain that way when Harry crested the ridge and raised a hand in greeting with a smile that was genuine and as warm as the day itself? I certainly found it hard to do so, but when I stood, the puckered letter from Ann in my pocket reminded me of why my thoughts were in contrast to the radiance of the day and the affection of his greeting. Yet, I couldn't help but smile when he enclosed me in those arms, strong and brown, honed by honest labour throughout these years of war, and I returned his embrace.

"It's good to see you, Johnny." He put his hands on my shoulders and stepped back, looking at me in his enquiring way and asked the obvious question.

"What the hell are we meeting *here* for? Home is down there, Johnny." He nodded back at the valley. "The war is over," he said softly.

I nodded. "I guess it is. It's just a matter of… what I do now." Before he could answer, I sat in the shadow of the rough cairn which dominated the small peak and said, "The three of us started this cairn… do you remember?"

Harry gave me an uncomfortable glance but said forthrightly enough, "Of course, I do, Johnny. Every time we climbed here, we placed one more stone."

He touched the cairn, and I knew his thoughts had swept back through the years to his young adulthood and beyond, when a dark-haired girl sat between us, laughing. At the same time, her very presence, as she grew into womanhood, restricted our thoughts and actions such that we were caught in a giddying, stultifying inaction. Then, the war came upon us.

"A lot of stones and an awful lot of dreaming." He paused. "I think you and I were dreaming of the same thing."

We fell silent. A single cloud passed overhead, and its shadow slid between us. It may just as well have been, as always, that of Ann.

"Where is she, Harry?" I did not want to feel angry, but that bitterness flared within me and gave rise to something heated, something that required actions to quell it.

I contemplated the 4 years of conflict which had been filled with an utter fear that grew at every aerial mission, albeit tempered scantly by the knowledge that I was not alone in the completeness of my fear. There were thousands of us, fighting on land and sea and in the air, enduring it because we had to, because it was right to do so.

Unfairly, I thought in a sullen way of Harry left here on the farm below, with Ann close by. Unfairly, because he had wanted to enlist but was not allowed to. The nation needed feeding, it was as important as any conscription, though he would not have thought so. To me, it seemed like an opportunity for him to become closer to Ann, to finally choose between us.

"I should have written." He spoke uneasily and turned to look out over those three counties as they stretched further and further away to meet a blue horizon.

"There was no need." I fumbled to take out the letter from my pocket, took it from the envelope, and unfolded it with fingers that had for some reason begun to shake. "She saved you the job."

"Oh?" he sounded surprised and looked back at me. "She said she wanted me to explain, she thought it best."

"What is there to explain? It's plain enough... It's not me that she loves." Her words, precise, clipped as though she could not bear to explain further, were written in that pastoral handwriting I had known since childhood.

Harry stepped closer to the edge of the mountain. He shielded his eyes to better see the farmhouse settled in the distance below, between the village and the variegated land beyond it. I felt him sigh rather than heard it– it was obscured because the silence was disturbed by the faintest of drones as a dark speck broke the bluest of skies as it flew towards us above the landscape.

I kept my voice steady, just, when I spoke, "Be happy, Harry, and make her happy too." As I said this, I knew that whatever he did or said next was important. I was not sure that I would be able to control my actions any more than I could the trembling of my hands.

He frowned and held out his hand. "Give me the letter, Johnny."

He took it, and turning his back to me, he read quickly. Incredulously, I heard him laugh, and at that, a dark mist shaded with red dropped before my eyes. He stood upon the highest crag, above an escarpment that dropped precipitously and dangerously. I walked towards him, and if another shadow had not glided between us, I cannot swear that I would not have pushed him into that abyss.

It was only then that I noticed the familiar engine growl above. The Avro Lancaster passed high overhead, distinctly profiled against the blue of the sky, and I stopped. I followed it with my eyes as it made its way, perhaps transporting British POWs home, perhaps even flying for the last time – its purpose well served. I recalled how I also had sat within such a plane, how I had flown high in battle, fierce and high, higher than the petty gods of jealousy and envy could fly; they remained inconsequently below in a tiny world that only became real once I had landed safely home.

With slow steps, I turned to make my way down the mountain.

"Johnny! Where the hell are you going?!"

I said, "Somewhere, Harry… away from you and Ann."

He shook his head fiercely, and then laughed again. "You bloody fool. Do you see my name in this letter?"

I had read the letter a dozen times. Dazedly, I realised that Harry was not mentioned once. "Well, no…" I finally said, "I just assumed…"

"Don't. Don't ever assume anything but madness and inconsistency in a world like this. I thought you would have learned that. She's gone, Johnny – just plain gone… she's outgrown us both."

He gripped me by both shoulders, then pulled me close. "You bloody, bloody fool," he whispered.

One day, we stood upon a mountain – my brother and I. There were no shadows between us as we looked silently out across three counties and at the village and the farmhouse far below. Laughing, we linked arms and began the long walk home.

THAT WHICH IS MIGHTY

The old man and his grandson stood beneath the African moon. It was huge and white and round, and its light slanted across a black treetop canopy that stretched farther and farther away towards a boundless horizon. From below came the sounds of scurrying, snuffling, lumbering, living forest life, which filtered up and across the ravine to where the pair stood.

To the old warrior, these sounds were ancient and eternal – a reminder of his own fleeting place in the arrangement of life, but the boy listened with some indifference. Then he heard the low, foreboding growl of Gyata the lion, and when Owea the tree bear raised a cry that prickled his skin, he placed his small hand in the other's, which was aged, worn and yet comforting to someone who had spent the first 7 years of his life in the city.

"Grandfather, why do we stand here?"

"Sshh…"

They listened again, and this time the boy heard the flowing waters of the river below, which spilled over and across undying rocks, rushing and gushing life towards his grandfather's village further along the valley; the trees undulated with a wind that gusted and sighed with the spirits of their ancestors and caused the elder to sigh in return. Kumi, a descendant of Osei Bonsu, he who had long ago led the mighty Asante to victory against the Fante, looked beyond the darkened village and across the valley to the distant hills where he knew the city lay in shrouded modernity, and with indifference to the past, resentful that his son had chosen to make that his future. He shook the boy off and frowned, though he knew it was unreasonable to do so.

"Your father comes to collect you in the morning…what have you learned in your time with me, Akosi?"

Akosi concentrated, he was not sure what his grandfather wanted to hear; he did not want to upset him, but his father had taught him to be honest about all matters, whether that be in the city of his birth or in the fields and forests of his forefathers.

He looked thoughtful and gazed beyond the river at the moon; it climbed imperceptibly into a clear sky speckled with a billion stars and a thought occurred to him.

"When you sit in your own house you learn nothing," he quoted the old proverb.

"Yes, yes, but WHAT have you learned?"

"I... I miss my friends and school..."

His grandfather uttered an impatient grunt and turned back towards the trees. Akosi followed with swift, small steps but which were still less silent than those of his grandfather. They left the echo of the turbulent river behind and, when they reached the rough-hewn clearing where they were to spend the night, Kumi lit a fire. In silence, they crouched and watched the flames as they crackled above the sound of the wind and snaked back and forth, ushering away the living darkness of the forest.

Kumi looked across at Akosi, then reached towards a bundle of bedding and from beneath it, pulled out a canvas wrap, a concession to the trappings of modern Ghanaian life, undid the drawstring, and stood up. He allowed the wrap to fall to the ground and what remained in his hands gleamed in yellow, white, and black ferocity – the full-length skin and head of Gyahene the leopard. Despite being lifeless and dormant, it retained a scornful savagery that matched its beauty, and Akosi's eyes widened – then noticing the leopard's unseeing eyes, a sadness came upon him, though he listened in fascination as his grandfather spoke.

He told the tale of how Gyahene had come upon Kumi's father many years ago, one evening when the sun had been red and low. Ha! Gyahene had been hungry and angry, his stomach aching after 4 days without food, and though it was with reluctance that he found himself face-to-face with a man, his irritability and hunger overpowered his natural aversion. He must eat! Kumi's father had stood on the edge of the very ravine that Akosi himself had looked out from this evening and Gyahene had sprung from behind, his jaws seeking the neck, as was his wont.

"My father was too quick. Ha! They wrestled until the sun hid and the moon took its place."

Akosi pursed his lips. "That long?"

Kumi smiled. "Well, perhaps not so long." Then, he grew serious

81

again. "They fought, Akosi, long and hard, and my father, with his bare hands, took the life of Gyahene; when it was done, my father lay spent alongside him. He pulled himself up, and for a moment thought that he would throw Gyahene out and into the ravine – but he considered how they had both fought with honour, and that was no end befitting one so noble. There lay that foe who lived majestically in the land we love; he died at the hands of a warrior and descendent of kings."

Kumi laid the fur on the ground; when placed in that manner, its great length was clearly visible, and Akosi marvelled at its splendour and at how his great-grandfather had overcome the leopard's ravenous rage.

Stretching himself on the floor, his back to the fire, Kumi closed his eyes; he felt some satisfaction now that Akosi had shown an interest in the forest and his ancestry, for what can be greater than honour?! He sighed, he muttered, and he slept.

He did not notice Akosi lift the fur from the floor and wrap it around himself, the head placed above his own. Tying it tightly about his person, Akosi thought to himself, "Now! Now I am Gyahene. I will see what it is like to be one with the forest!"

*

Kumi dreamed. He was his father, he was Osei – he was both at once, and Gyahene rose before him in his fierce magnificence, snarling. Yet, he was not afraid. He stood, and he rose above the beast. *Now you shall see what a warrior can do! Ha! Run Gyahene, run!* Gyahene turned, and bounded away with sleek swiftness as the warrior pursued him with a fleetness of foot such that he barely touched the ground.

They reached the ravine; the moon seemed to stand still above them both, and the leopard turned seemingly small and inconsequential. The warrior picked him up and raised him above his head. *Where is your fight Gyahene?! Ha! There is no honour in this.* He threw the mewling beast up and out where it spat and cried weakly as it turned and turned, flailing as it plunged towards the river that rumbled below.

*

Kumi woke up. He found himself standing alone, looking out across the ravine; the sky was still clear, the stars still numbered a billion, and the moon still bathed everything in its silver glory. He shook his head. Then, he recalled his dream and his skin went cold. He shook violently and sank to his knees.

"Akosi…" he whispered.

He lay prone and peered down into the valley where the occasional gleam marked the course of the river as it tumbled onwards.

"Akosi!!"

There was no answer, but only his own voice echoed, as it trembled and reverberated across and back along the valley. He knelt and hugged himself with grief and bitterness at his own pride.

"Grandfather?"

His eyes wide and white, Kumi turned, and Akosi walked towards him, carrying Gyahene.

"Grandfather, I have been thinking alone. I have learned that *'a straight tree never lasts in the forest',*" he quoted again. "I can be part of the city, AND I can be part of the forest if I so wish."

"That is a good lesson to learn, Akosi," he whispered. "But I have learned a better one. Love is greater than honour. It is mightier than warriors and more powerful than kings and nobler than foolish pride."

He pulled Akosi close to his chest and hugged him as his eyes filled, and the moon looked down upon them both with approval.

About the Author

C.G. Harris is a lover of stories, both reading and writing them from his home in Kent. He has a wife, two daughters, four grandchildren, one cat and one dog.

In between writing, he enjoys playing the guitar and ukulele, juggling, and tap dancing...although not necessarily all at the same time.

Light and Dark is his first published book of short stories. He has since written a second collection (*Kisses from the Sun*) and a book of detective stories featuring Aaron Baum the Manhattan P.I.

He is now working on his novel *Billy's Band* about a rock band based in and around the streets of Brixton and Stockwell where he grew up.

For more information, his books, extracts and latest news visit his web site: *www.cgharrisauthor.com*

L - #0125 - 060623 - C0 - 210/148/5 - PB - DID3598856